HERBIE GOES TO MONTE CARLO

Herbie Goes to Monte Carlo

Adapted from Walt Disney Productions'
screen presentation

by JOHN HARVEY

Illustrated by Tony Masero

NEW ENGLISH LIBRARY
TIMES MIRROR

NEL Books are published by
New English Library Limited from Barnard's Inn, Holborn, London EC1N 2JR
Made and printed in Great Britain by Hunt Barnard Printing Ltd, Aylesbury, Bucks

45003651 0

HERBIE GOES TO MONTE CARLO

CHAPTER ONE

The car drove off the ship and joined one of the queues that led towards the French customs sheds. An ordinary car to look at, one which would not usually be given a second glance. Only this time there were racing numbers painted on its body and on a car such as this one they looked – well, to put it kindly – a little out of place.

The queue moved slowly forward until the car finally drew level with the customs post. The uniformed figure stepped up to it and reached out a hand towards the driver's window.

He accepted the three passports and stood back to examine them carefully.

The picture on the first showed a handsome face, obviously American, with clean-cut features and lively, attractive eyes. A man in his late twenties to early thirties. The Frenchman squinted into the car. Yes, he thought, a sportsman by the look of him. And quite a ladies' man, too.

'Jim Douglas', the passport read.

'*Merci*, Monsieur.' The man handed the freshly stamped passport back through the window and opened the second.

'Wheely Appleyard'. The names these Americans had!

This one appeared to be a good ten or fifteen years older. His face was lined and had a rather surprised expression, as if the photographer had sneaked up on him to take his passport picture. Here again, though, there was a sign of humour in the eyes. He seemed friendly, kind, possibly a little impetuous.

The official stamped the passport and returned it. Now for the third.

The third!

The customs man took a few more paces backwards and bumped against the wall of his hut. He wiped at his forehead and took a pair of spectacles from his inside pocket.

Yes. There was no doubting it – the picture that was meant to show the passport holder was of a small car, an insignificant-looking car. A Volkswagen Beetle.

He went up to the car and put his head through the open window. 'Monsieur, I think you make some kind of joke, no?'

'No.'

'But, Monsieur, this is like a . . . like a passport for a . . . a car.'

'That's right,' agreed the driver. 'That's Herbie's passport.'

The customs man stood up, rather too quickly, and banged his head against the top edge of the window.

'Ow! Ooh! *Mon dieu*! This is impossible! You cannot have a passport for a car.'

'Well,' said Jim Douglas, leaning out, 'you can see that it isn't impossible at all. It's there in your hand. All stamped and signed.'

'Signed!' cried the customs man, one hand to his head in amazement.

8

'Of course, Herbie can't write his own name.'

'Oh, I am so pleased to hear that!'

'But he made his mark, you see, just there.'

'The car made his mark?'

'Sure with his front wheel. Tyre treads are as in-dividual as handwriting, you know.'

'Say,' interrupted Wheely, leaning over, 'can we get all stamped up and out of here? We've got to get to Paris as soon as possible.'

'*Oui, Monsieur*,' agreed the customs man, who was looking more than a little pale by now. 'Anything to get rid . . . er, anything to help you on your journey.'

'Good, that's great.'

'It's only that it is not usual in our country to give a passport to an ordinary car.'

'This,' said Wheely loudly, 'is no ordinary car. This is Herbie. Ain't it, Herbie?'

And the car honked its horn of its own accord.

'Herbie?' asked the official.

'That's right,' said Jim. 'See, the name's right there under the photo. You see,' he confided, 'Herbie's more like a person than a car.' He patted the steering wheel affectionately and looked at the customs man, who hastily stamped Herbie's passport, took a final look at it, then handed it back through the car window.

'Thanks a lot,' smiled Jim, and let the car into gear.

'Yes, thanks,' echoed Wheely.

The French official was too dumbfounded to say any-thing. He simply stood there and watched as the little Volkswagen drove away towards the port exit. There was something else that he'd noticed when he'd taken that final glance at the photograph. He could have sworn that, like his owners, the car had had a distinct grin on its face!

Several hours later Herbie was not smiling at all. Far from it. He was stuck in the biggest traffic jam he'd encountered since trying to go round Times Square in the wrong direction at five on a Friday afternoon. Not only that, it was so noisy!

All of the other cars were burping and honking their horns, so that it was like being in the middle of a symphony orchestra with every player blowing or bowing with all his might and all playing a different tune.

Herbie was getting a headache!

Jim and Wheely weren't feeling much better.

Wheely had a large coloured map of Paris open on his lap and was doing his best to unravel the whys and wherefores of that city. It wasn't easy. And there were so many one-way systems and so much other traffic that it was becoming more or less impossible.

'Well,' said Jim, 'you're supposed to be the navigator on this trip. Where are we?'

Wheely peered at the map and struggled through the directions in very hesitant French: '*Rue Boissière à Rue de Lubek à droit à Place d'Iena.*'

Jim glanced across in exasperation. 'Wheely, will you give it to me in English?'

'Sure,' replied Wheely, turning towards the driver. 'We're lost.'

Jim's face showed something close to despair, but Herbie was not about to give up so easily. The steering wheel suddenly pulled out of Jim's hands and swung sharply to the left.

'Hey! Herbie!'

'What's he doing?' called Wheely, alarmed.

Herbie crossed and recrossed the streams of traffic, fishtailing between brake light and brake light, ignoring the shouts and honks of protest. The little car made a screeching U-turn and pulled to a juddering halt next to a *gendarme* who was directing traffic in the centre of a large crossroads.

Jim turned to Wheely. 'He's getting us *un*-lost.' He patted the wheel. 'Thanks, Herbie.'

Meanwhile, the *gendarme* was continuing to whistle and make fierce gestures with his truncheon, casting occasional glances down at the strange car.

'Excuse me,' said Jim, sticking his head through the window. 'We're looking for the Trans-France Race Exposition.'

'*Ah, oui, oui,*' replied the *gendarme* and began to point with his stick. 'The first street to the left. That is going to be some race.'

'Well,' put in Wheely with some pride, 'you're looking at the winner right now.'

Wheely gave Herbie a pat and the *gendarme* looked at the two Americans and their car in disbelief.

'This car??' he roared. 'The winner??'

The French policeman bellowed with laughter and turned to walk round Herbie. As he passed the rear, a jet of black oil squirted out and ran down his trouser leg. The *gendarme* became aware of a nasty sticky feeling and looked slowly down.

He stood there in dismay with traffic rushing round him on all sides, too astonished to do anything about the Volkswagen that was following his instructions and making for the exposition.

The route took Herbie along a narrow cobbled street that was almost blocked by a large truck. Herbie was only just able to squeeze past, and headed for a large square at the far end.

Once the little car had passed, two armed security guards carrying pistols got out of the truck. They were joined by an immaculately dressed man, short in stature and gazing very nervously about himself. This was

11

Monsieur Ribeaux, the curator of the museum to which the guards were making a very important delivery.

He was wearing a dark three-piece suit over a dazzling white shirt and a spotted tie. He fidgeted with his glasses and brushed his fingers through his thinning hair as the guards let two more security men out of the rear of the truck. They were carrying a strong box – the object of all the preparations and precautions.

'Huh!' said a spectator. 'All of this for the museum payroll?'

Ribeaux heard the remark and turned on the man indignantly. 'For the most magnificent diamond in the world, Monsieur. *L'Etoile de Joie.* The Star of Joy.'

'Could we have a little peek?' asked one of the others gathered close by.

Ribeaux raised both hands: 'This afternoon, at one o'clock precisely, Monsieur, you and all of Paris will be able to take that "peek". Now stand back.'

He turned away and began to walk towards the entrance. The two guards carried the strong box into the museum, with the pair of armed men flanking them on either side.

Monsieur Ribeaux was not a man to take chances. Oh, no!

In the square in front of the Eiffel Tower a large crowd had gathered for an exposition to publicise the new Trans-France Motor Race. Streamers, banners and posters decorated the square and scattered about it were the dozen or so racing cars that were going to take part. Close by the cars stood their proud drivers, all wearing the brightly coloured driving suits they would wear during the race itself.

The racing enthusiasts who had gathered there in the

Paris sunshine milled about between the cars, bending to examine the cars' finer points or stopping to chat with the drivers.

The master of ceremonies moved through the crowd, going from one entry to the next. Everywhere he went he was followed by a small television crew who were covering the action.

They stopped by a tall, handsome driver wearing a red suit.

' . . . and, fresh from his triumphs on the European racing circuit, Bruno Von Stickle, who will be driving his Lazer 917 GT coupé.'

Von Stickle smiled – rather, smirked – and bowed to the applauding crowd.

The MC looked round, in search of something new, and saw . . .

'Ah, ha! I see the American entry, Jim Douglas, is just arriving. He will be racing in . . . uh . . . in a most unusual entry.'

Some of the crowd looked in surprise as Herbie slowly drove into the centre of the space with Jim and Wheely in the front seats. As soon as they realised that the little car was one of the competitors, up against the other powerful sports cars, they began to call to one another and laugh out loud.

'Something funny must have happened,' said Wheely as he got out.

Jim nodded wryly. 'I think it's us.'

The MC came towards them, the camera crew following closely. 'How about giving Jim Douglas and his partner, Wheely Applegate, a nice warm Paris welcome?'

The crowd responded generously: the only ones not applauding were the German driver, Von Stickle, and his closest rival, Claude Gilbert, who stood next to his powerful Pantera II.

'This little car,' the MC went on, pointing to Herbie, 'has been the toast of America.' He looked quickly at his notes. 'Let's see, when was your last win?'

'Twelve years ago,' replied Jim, rather quietly.

Once again the crowd burst into laughter.

With annoyance, Wheely grabbed the microphone. 'That was only 'cause that was our last race!'

Jim grinned and took the mike from him. 'We're making a kind of a "comeback",' he told the crowd. 'That's why being in this race is so important to all of us. Of course, we won't be coming back very far if we don't qualify first.'

The French crowd applauded Jim's spirit, although none of them, looking at Herbie, could believe that they would finish anywhere near first – if they finished at all.

'Qualify!' exclaimed Wheely. 'Are you kidding? Don't let his modesty fool you, folks, or the fact that this little car is just coming out of retirement. Why, you won't find a finer tuned, cleaner engine anywhere.'

'Of course,' agreed Bruno Von Stickle, 'it must be easy to keep clean. You just drop it into the washing machine along with your socks.'

Wheely took the joke as well as he could. 'I appreciate your humour. But just don't you worry about this little washing machine . . . uh, car. It's a real jewel!'

At that very moment, the real jewel was resting on a small velvet pillow inside the museum. The diamond glistened brilliantly in the light, sparkles of dazzling strength coming from its many facets.

The pillow was resting on a special pedestal which had been put up in the centre of the small room in which the Star of Joy was the main exhibit. A number of fine paintings and statues lined the walls and two armed

14

guards stood between them and the jewel.

Close enough to be able to reach out and touch it was Monsieur Ribeaux. He was carefully explaining about the security system to a hand-picked museum guard.

Ribeaux took a small calculator-like computer from his pocket, extended an antenna attached to it and looked earnestly at a small notebook in his free hand.

'Here we have the finest security system that can be devised – and its secrets are all in this computer.'

He punched a number of buttons and looked up, satisfied with his efforts. 'Now . . . this alone would keep the diamond safe from the grasp of a thief.'

But the museum guard was both puzzled and worried about the responsibility. 'But Monsieur, one would only have to reach in and . . . you see, I have it!'

As his fingers touched the diamond an alarm rang

loudly. Ribeaux grabbed hold of him and threw the pair of them to the floor and out of the way as a large iron cage came crashing down from a trap-door in the ceiling.

The guard was astonished, but Ribeaux got up calmly enough, pleased with the demonstration of his security arrangements. 'The pillow is sensitive to the heat of any hand that gets too close to the diamond,' he explained. Then, pushing more buttons, he sent the cage back into the ceiling.

Ribeaux took a bell jar from the side of the room and placed it over both pillow and diamond. Stepping back, he then punched more buttons on the computer.

'What does that do?' asked the guard, still shaken.

'I am engaging a system of electric eye beams that surrounds the pedestal.'

'Beams?' said the guard, perplexed. 'I don't see any b...'

He reached out his hand towards one of the posts and the alarm was triggered off again. With a great ringing sound filling the room, the cage came crashing down once again.

Pleased that he had demonstrated the efficiency of his system, Ribeaux ushered the three men out of the room. 'One last precaution, gentlemen. If you will please step out of the room...'

In the hallway, Ribeaux punched a final set of buttons. 'Now the entire floor around the diamond is a trap,' he explained. 'Even the ash from a cigar would activate the alarm. So, my friend, how little you have to worry about.'

He clapped the museum guard on the shoulder and the guard managed to smile weakly back – perhaps it wasn't going to be as dangerous or difficult a job as he had thought.

What he did not know was that although he and the others had left the room, it was far from empty. For, only moments later, the two statues directly behind the pedestal opened up and very slowly and cautiously two men peered out.

They looked at each other, then at the diamond, then back towards each other again – and smiled.

Carefully they stepped out from inside the hollowed-out statues where they had been hiding. The first of them was a little man with big, big ideas. One of the best-known jewel thieves in the business!

He was smartly dressed as befitted a professional man – a three-piece suit and a natty red bow tie, a watch chain dangling from his waistcoat. He had a clipped moustache and short, well-brushed hair – the perfect picture of a businessman spending his day off at the museum.

Max's companion – for Max was the smart man's name – was far from elegant or well-dressed. Quincey was twice as big as his friend and twice as ugly.

He was wearing a shabby old overcoat over a pair of baggy trousers and a dirty roll-neck sweater. On his head perched a cloth cap.

Max took out his watch and checked it: 'Right on schedule.' He slipped the watch back and rubbed his hands. 'Ten steps to a lovely six million dollars.'

'Or one step to Devil's Island if anything touches the floor, eh?'

Quincey unrolled a length of nylon rope from around his large middle and lassoed a huge bronze statue at the far side of the room. That done, he tied the remaining end to a pillar behind where he was standing and pulled it taut.

It stretched directly over the bell jar containing the diamond and avoided breaking any of the radar beams. Perfect, Quincey thought.

But Max was not so impressed.

'Patience, Quincey,' he urged, taking a small notebook

2

out of his pocket. 'Electronics has the answer. This note-book is our passport to the future.'

Quincey was a simple soul who didn't trust what he didn't understand. For years he'd refused to put slices of bread into his old mum's toaster because he couldn't see exactly what happened to it when it was in there.

'Thanks,' he said, 'but I'd rather put my trust in this bit of rope.'

With one mighty bound – in truth, it wasn't very mighty, but for a man of Quincey's size, it was a fair effort – the cloth-capped figure was clinging to the rope and starting to swing across the room.

Max watched for a moment, but soon got bored with his colleague's tortured efforts. He took out a small computer like the one the museum curator had been using and started to make similar calculations.

'When the man has it all worked out for us,' said Max, 'it's silly not to use it.' He pressed a few more digits and walked over towards the bell-jar containing the diamond. Quincey got down gingerly from the rope and walked over towards him, astounded that each step on the floor didn't set off alarms and fetch armed guards from all directions.

Still looking suspiciously around he took out a spray-can from his inside pocket and squirted the area between the posts.

'What the ... ?'

'Just wanted to check for the radar beam.'

'But ...'

'There!' Quincey grinned as the spray made a beam obvious. 'There it is!'

'Yes,' Max agreed, 'but ... ' and he pressed digits on his computer with a smug expression, ' ... there it isn't!'

And the radar beam disappeared.

'Science has the answer, my friend. Science and what

the man told us beforehand.' At the mention of the man, Max winked knowingly at Quincey, who tried to wink back, but didn't quite manage it. There was something about the man that frightened him.

'Just watch me.'

Whereupon Max strode between the posts and went towards the pedestal. Quincey watched nervously, one eye firmly closed, as Max lifted up the bell jar and both men saw the diamond sparkling at them from its perch on the velvet cushion.

'Some hunk of rock!' exclaimed Quincey, now daring to use both.

'You could live a lifetime without setting your eyes on a rock like that. Never mind actually setting your hands on it.'

It was enough to make Quincey's eyes water. He started to reach forward to the pedestal, not thinking of the consequences.

'No, Quincey! Patience, patience! Don't you see the pillow's the trap. One more set of numbers. Just a second and . . . and . . . and . . . '

'Come on! I thought you said just one more lot of them numbers of yours.'

'So I did, but . . . '

'But what?'

'I can't read the man's figures.'

'Double X, you mean?'

'Sssh!' Max put a finger to his lips and glared at Quincey. 'Don't even say the man's name.'

'But I didn't say his name. I said D . . . '

'Exactly!'

Poor Quincey! He wiped his brow and looked at the floor. He never would understand these blokes who'd been to university. The best he'd ever managed was

Hatfield Polytechnic – working as a brickie on the extension to the library.

Max was still puzzling over the figure. Was it an 0 or a 6, or even a 9? It could be the difference between success and failure. Between – he paused to tug nervously at the skin at his throat and thought about the way the man would look on their making a mess of the operation – life and death!

'Don't worry your head about that stuff,' said Quincey, 'I came prepared.'

From yet another pocket inside his large and dirty overcoat he drew forth an accordion-like mechanical claw and patted it, smiling. 'The old ways are still the best ways.'

'All right,' Max agreed. 'But you've got six minutes till the guard checks the room. Get on with it!'

Quincey extended the mechanical arm and slowly and carefully moved it towards the pillow. He manoeuvred it over the diamond and opened the claw. Quincey was sweating and blinking as it dripped from his forehead on to his eyelids. Close to him, unable to take his eyes off the diamond, Max was perspiring also; he wanted to check the time on his watch, but couldn't bring himself to do so.

The claw closed around the sparkling stone.

The two thieves chanced a hasty glance at each other.

Neither of them could believe it – the world's largest and most expensive diamond in their grasp at . . .

There was a small but definite alarm-like ringing and Quincey let the diamond fall back out of the claw and stared at Max in dismay. For several seconds Max was frozen with fear: and then he realised exactly where the ringing was coming from. He guiltily reached into one of his pockets and took out a watch with a built-in alarm.

As he pressed the knob to switch it off, Quincey stared

at his friend in amazement. 'I thought you'd got that thing fixed?'

'So,' gulped Max, 'did I.'

He wiped away the sweat and looked at the watch face. 'We've still got two minutes.'

Quincey nodded and moved the claw back over the diamond. But such was his nervousness that he could not hold the instrument still enough to pick up the precious stone.

Max elbowed the bigger man out of the way and took over. Still the diamond seemed to resist their attempts to capture it. Quincey watched, gnashing his teeth noisily.

'Almost had it. One more try . . .'

'There's no time!' shouted Quincey, checking the watch. 'That guard's practically at the door.'

'You want the diamond, don't you?' demanded Max angrily.

'Yes, and there's only one way we're ever going to get it.' Quincey gave up all attempts to be careful and thrust his hand towards the pillow and grabbed the stone. Immediately the alarm went off. The cage appeared out of the trap-door in the ceiling and hurtled down towards the men. Down, down, d . . .

The rope that Quincey had stretched across the room broke its descent.

Quincey and Max stared at each other, at the cage hovering over their heads, then back at their own frightened faces once more.

'There's only one thing to do in a situation like this.'

Quincey nodded: 'Right.'

And stride for stride they dashed towards one of the windows at the rear of the room, dived headlong through the plate glass and rolled on to the lawn outside.

At that precise moment the door opened to reveal the

museum curator and the guard. The two of them ran to the pedestal and looked in shock and horror at the black velvet pillow. No diamond!

'*Diable*!' yelled Ribeaux to the statues that surrounded the room.

'*C'est terrible. Terrible!*'

The statues looked singularly unimpressed.

Ribeaux pulled at his hair, stamped first his right foot, then his left, and finally began jumping up and down.

The impact of Ribeaux's leaps together with the weight of the cage finally snapped the rope. The cage plummetted to the ground, neatly trapping both him and the guard inside it, helpless.

CHAPTER TWO

Jim was feeling pretty good. The sun was shining; the sky was blue; the crowds were showing a lot of interest in the race in general and in his little car in particular. Either side of the street leading into the square was lined with white balloons advertising the Trans-France Race.

Yes, sir, if Herbie pulled out what Jim thought he was capable of, then they were in with a chance. More than just a chance, a ...

'Hey!'

Jim had been thinking so hard about the race that he hadn't noticed where he was going. Not that he'd walked into a tree, nor a lamp-post, not even a litter bin or one of those pillars plastered with advertisements. None of those things would have shouted at him like that. That much was certain.

Nor would they have had the very pleasing shape that Jim had barged into. They would not have been wearing a racing outfit, or have had such lovely long red hair.

'Hey, where d'you think you're going?' The girl stooped down to pick up her crash helmet.

'Monte Carlo?' Jim suggested.

'Very funny!' she snapped, straightening up.

He made a half smile and bent to pick up the helmet himself; unfortunately the girl did exactly the same thing at the same time. You can guess what happened.

Yes, that's right. Two pairs of hands rubbing two sore heads.

'Sorry,' Jim said after a few painful moments. 'I was just trying to prove that the age of chivalry isn't dead.'

'Maybe not. But another bump like that and one of us might be.'

Jim handed her the helmet. 'Perhaps you ought to be wearing this instead of your boyfriend.'

She did not look pleased. 'What boyfriend? This is mine.'

Jim nodded. 'I was only teasing. My next line was going to be "haven't I seen you somewhere before?" And I have. On the sports page. Diane Darcy. Dover Speedway. Ran a whale of a race last month.'

'Thanks,' said Diane, looking almost pleased.

'Finished third. That was really great.'

' "For a woman".'

'I didn't say that.'

'No. But try to tell me you weren't thinking of me just as a woman.'

This time Jim's smile was broader. 'Guilty there . . . but not "just" a woman . . . '

'Uh, Jim . . . '

Jim turned quickly on hearing Wheely's voice from behind. A little too quickly. His arm knocked Diane's crash helmet from her hand. The two of them started to bend then stopped, warily. Wheely stepped in between them, picked up the helmet and handed it to the girl. She nodded her thanks and walked off – careful not to look at Jim.

Wheely put his arm round Jim and spoke to him confidentially, like a wise old uncle. 'Just a word. Paris may be the land of love . . . but it can also be the land of heart-break. I'll make a deal with you. I'm willing to resist the girls if you are.'

Jim turned to look at Wheely's rather battered face and his none too attractive clothes. Whereas *he* usually smiled back from the mirror quite handsomely, and was wearing a new leather jacket, a clean check shirt and a smart beige cap.

'That's some deal,' he said. 'That's some sacrifice.'

'Yeah, but I'm willing to make it.'

They were back by Herbie when a fresh announcement came over the loudspeaker system. 'May I have your attention please. Those drivers who are in the qualifying rounds this afternoon will be leaving in ten minutes.'

The arrogant Bruno strolled towards them, a smug smile all over his face. 'Will you be qualifying at the track, Douglas? Or only in your friend's imagination?'

Wheely was going to give him a piece of his mind – he had plenty spare – but Jim stopped him and calmed him down. 'You just keep your eyes on this little car,' he said to Bruno. 'You're in for a few surprises.'

Bruno smirked and stared down his nose at Herbie.

Little did he know Herbie was staring back at him – and that he didn't like what he saw. Right, Herbie thought, I'm going to wash that grin right off your face. Herbie moved one of the water sprayers below his wind-screen until it was pointing directly at Bruno's face.

Ready!

Steady!

Flow!

Bruno jumped back as a jet of water hit him in the eye. He wiped his hand across his face and stared wildly round, not knowing where it had come from. Wheely, however, was clued-up on most of Herbie's tricks. He leaned down and patted him on the bonnet.

'Attaboy, Herbie. You just saved that Bruno from a terrible beating!'

Before Bruno could do or say anything further, there was the sound of sirens and the squealing of brakes. Several police cars appeared at different sides of the square and a number of armed *gendarmes* jumped out and hurried into the crowd.

The police were in time to stop the two thieves getting out of the square, where they had gone after escaping through the museum window.

Max and Quincey backed into the thick of the crowd, doing their best not to look suspicious.

'Attention, everybody. Nobody is to leave the area. I repeat, no one is to leave the area.'

A rumble of excitement and concern ran through the crowd. Jim was anxious about getting Herbie away from the square in time to enter the qualifying heats at the race track. The last thing he wanted was to get involved in something that would prevent them from even starting the race. Heaven knows, finishing it was going to be difficult enough.

The policeman had the megaphone to his lips again: 'Ladies and gentlemen, do not be alarmed. There has been a theft at the museum close by. Everyone will have to be searched before leaving the area.'

Jim raised his hands and walked up to the police chief. 'Might as well start with us. We've got a race to catch.'

While Jim and Wheely and the other drivers were being searched, Max and Quincey were trying to back through the crowd and slip out at the far side. But they realised that the cordon of police left no loopholes.

'No sense in us both being caught,' smiled Quincey painfully, taking the diamond from his pocket, and shook hands with his partner.

Max was not pleased to find that on taking his hand

away, the diamond was inside his palm. In a normal situation he would have been only too pleased. But this one was getting less and less normal every second.

Even then a very large *gendarme* was approaching with an expression which suggested that if he found the stone on Max's person, he would personally administer the necessary punishment before trial.

Max backed away until something solid stopped him. He felt behind him and realised it was a car; felt further and there was something round underneath his fingers; something round that turned to the left – turned and came away.

A petrol cap. Which meant . . .

Max smiled when he had thought he might never smile again: and dropped the diamond into the petrol tank.

'No need for either of us to get caught,' he beamed, and put up his arms for the *gendarme* to search him.

From the corner of his eye he could see that the car he had popped the diamond into was a strange little car indeed for one that was going to take part in a race. Easy to remember, though, and obviously simple to remove the stone from when . . .

Max became pale. Quincey caught his arm, thinking his friend was going to faint. It was the sight of Jim and Wheely getting into the car and starting to drive it away as quickly as they could.

Quincey took off his cap and screwed it up. 'We may never see it again!' he moaned.

'Don't worry,' said the MC, who was passing by at the time, 'you need only wait till four o'clock this afternoon. Then you can see that car and most of the others in a showroom on the Champs Elysées.'

Quincey and Max nodded and grinned: things were not turning out quite so badly for them after all.

For Monsieur Ribeaux, the curator of the museum, things had turned out very badly indeed. To lose the most expensive stone in the world on its first afternoon in his custody! It was too much! Thousands and thousands of pounds too much.

Nor was Ribeaux the only gloomy person in the room. Seated behind the desk was one of France's finest detectives. A man who had solved more crimes than all the rest of the Paris force put together. A policeman of the highest reputation and influence.

The famous Inspector Bouchet.

He sat behind his desk, scowling at the museum curator. A foolproof system which they had worked out together in order to keep the diamond safe and now ...

The Inspector sighed and rolled his eyes in his round face. He twitched the ends of his moustache, removed his spectacles and put them back on again without so much as a wipe. He brushed a hand back through his grey hair. He pushed another hand into a pocket of his blue raincoat and came up with – nothing. Not even a used ticket for the metro.

Bouchet continued to sit there, clueless.

Ribeaux stared at the helpless expression on the great Inspector's face and burst into tears.

'Please, Monsieur Ribeaux, you must stop crying.'

'If I stop crying,' the curator replied tearfully, 'I shall kill myself.'

At that the third person in the room stepped forward with a cheery smile and a handkerchief. 'I assure you, Monsieur, that will not be necessary.'

The smile and the handkerchief belonged to a young policeman called Fontenoy, who had been assigned to help Inspector Bouchet on this difficult case. The Inspector was his idol and he was going to do his best to impress the older policeman.

'Inspector Bouchet will have that diamond back for you like that.' And Fontenoy snapped his fingers in Ribeaux's face.

The Inspector sighed; all of this youthful enthusiasm was getting him down – and the case was scarcely an hour old.

'Thank you for your confidence, Fontenoy, but I'm afraid I'll require just a bit more time.'

This was too much for Ribeaux. Tears left his eyes as quickly as the diamond had left his museum. 'Every moment that passes could be taking the diamond further away.'

But Fontenoy, with the persistent good cheer of the young – or the less than sane – would have nothing of this pessimism.

'No, no, Monsieur! Every moment that passes will be bringing the Inspector closer to the solution.'

Ribeaux was almost on his knees. Fontenoy was leaning over him, trying to dab his eyes dry. From his desk, it seemed to the Inspector that the two of them were about to perform some strange dance.

'You have nothing to fear.' Fontenoy was saying. 'With a man of Inspector Bouchet's experience and reputation ...'

'Reputation!?' The museum curator was aghast. 'Do you know where my reputation is? I'll tell you where it is. Twenty-five years out of the window with that diamond!'

The Inspector could stand it no longer. He stood up, straightened his raincoat, and stared at the two men. 'Please control yourselves, gentlemen. And you, Monsieur – this robbery was carefully conceived, but we will do everything within our power to put the diamond safely back in your hands.'

Ribeaux stood there, twisting the handkerchief between his clenched fists, doubtless wishing it were the necks of the thieves who had run off with his precious diamond.

'Oh, if only I could believe you! If I could only believe you!!'

Whereupon, he ripped the handkerchief in half, sniffed and self-consciously offered the shredded halves to Fontenoy.

At that very moment, something else important was about to begin. At the Serpentine track, the qualifying rounds of the Trans-France Race was about to commence. The sun shone brightly on the various banners and balloons which decorated the grandstand where the cars were lined up. High-powered Ferraris, Lamborghinis and Porsches, as well as Triumphs and MGs – every one a shining, well-tuned example of the modern racing motor.

It was past this line that Jim Douglas drove Herbie.

The other drivers were still having difficulty in getting used to the idea of the little Beetle as a serious challenger for the race. So was the official when Jim approached him and gave his name.

But the race official checked his smile and then the clipboard he was holding. 'Yes, Mr Douglas. You're in the heat following this one. Good luck.'

Bruno called out from close by where his car was being given a final service. 'That's the same heat I'm in, Douglas, and good luck is more than you're going to be needing. You're going to be needing wings. I'm sending you and your four-wheel relic back to your rocking chairs.'

He picked up a hose, ready to put water into the radiator. Wheely came over to him and sneered: 'You may be in for a surprise.'

'Huh, I've seen your surprises,' Bruno replied, looking

at Herbie as if he had that second emerged from under a stone, 'and they *are little*!'

Herbie wasn't taking that!

He rolled backwards until one of his tyres was on the hose pipe. Abruptly the flow of water stopped. Amazed, Bruno lifted up the end of the hose and stared down it. When his face was close enough, Herbie rolled smartly back off the pipe. Immediately, water blasted into Bruno's face. He pulled the hose away and it streamed all over him.

'How about that?' asked Jim. 'And you can count on an even bigger surprise when the race starts.'

Little did Jim know it, but the surprises were going to be even stranger than he could anticipate.

It all began on the way past the pits. Herbie was going in one direction and a sleek Lancia appeared going in the other. Herbie looked, blinked, looked again. It was amazing! Fantastic! He had never seen anything – anyone – as beautiful in all his little life.

His wheels turned at a right angle and he began to follow the lovely car as it went towards the starting line. Jim did his best to get the steering back into order; Wheely worried and wondered what could have gone wrong with the mechanism.

But neither of them gave a thought to Herbie's heart!

One moment the Lancia was on the starting line with the other cars trying to qualify in the first heat, the next the official had brought down the flag and the race was on. The Lancia steamed away into the lead looking as if none of the other entrants could catch it.

None of them could. But Herbie . . . !

The Volkswagen reared up on its hind wheels, throwing Jim and Wheely back in their seats. The little car swung round a guard rail and raced down the track after the other cars.

'Herbie!' yelled Jim. 'Where are you going?'

At the moment straight ahead, and fast. Herbie zoomed past the back of the field then started to zig-zag between the rest of the cars, doing his best to catch up with the Lancia.

Jim did his best to bring Herbie under control. He changed gear. He put on the brake. Nothing worked.

'Herbie! Darn it, Herbie, you could get us disqualified.'

'Disqualified!' said Wheely. 'He could get us killed!'

But Herbie wasn't paying any attention, his thoughts were up ahead. Ahead, then alongside. He had caught the Lancia up. But this wasn't enough. Herbie started to move closer and closer to the other car, getting so close that Jim and Wheely thought they must crash into it.

The Lancia driver tried to wave the Beetle off and Jim signalled that he was doing his best. But there was no stopping Herbie now. He was going to make sure that she noticed him and no mistake. He made his windscreen wipers flap backwards and forwards, his ariel zip up and down and his horn emit a wavering sound that was the Herbie version of a wolf whistle.

Jim and Wheely looked at one another, amazed.

'What was that?' asked Wheely.

'I think you got him tuned up too fine.'

Herbie gave another wolf whistle. This time he got through to his objective. The Lancia blinked the hoods of her headlights seductively.

At that Herbie's radio came on and began to play a slow, romantic waltz.

'Herbie! Forget the music!'

Jim reached out and switched the radio off, but a second later it came back on again of its own accord. Herbie, inspired by the music, moved in front of the Lancia and began swaying around all over the track, waltzing in a zig-zagging motion that had Jim and

35

Wheely close to car-sickness and heart failure at the same time.

Three-four time, that is.

One, two, three; one, two, three . . .

'Herbie! Are you flipping your lid?'

Wheely grabbed at Jim's arm. 'Don't give him any more ideas!'

Herbie had more than enough ideas of his own, thank you very much. He made his dancing more and more energetic, throwing his body into the rhythm.

Behind him, the Lancia was zig-zagging too, but not because the car wanted to dance, but because its driver was desperately trying to get past the Beetle and get on with the race.

Skilful as the driver's manoeuvring was, Herbie's would have won a prize on 'Come Dancing'.

'He's out of his mind!' shouted Jim as he was thrown across the car.

'He's out of his mind, all right,' Wheely agreed. 'Over that luscious little Lancia.'

Jim looked at Wheely as though his partner had suddenly gone crazy as well. Cars shot past them on either side as the other entrants caught up and took the opportunity to leave the Lancia behind.

Herbie went into a spin that sent the car round in a full circle and ended up nose to nose with the Lancia and waltzing backwards.

'I'm telling you,' Wheely insisted, 'Paris and women have got him. I'm going to have to warn him the way I did you about that girl who dropped her helmet in your path like a handkerchief – like driver, like car!'

Jim didn't like the sound of what Wheely was saying. Not at all. But the sense of it was seeping through. After all, hadn't he been the one who'd always claimed that

Herbie was more than a mere car. That Herbie was almost human.

And whoever or whatever was human had to have a heart.

The Lancia slowed down and pulled off the track, the driver realising that the race was lost; the others were too far ahead now for there to be any chance of catching up.

Herbie slowed as well and came to a stop right alongside the Lancia.

Wheely scrambled out of the passenger door, his body continuing to waltz around dizzily to the rhythm of the car radio. Jim finally turned the music off and Wheely came to an unsteady halt.

The driver of the Lancia threw open the car door and jumped out, clad in a white suit with blue markings which contrasted with the yellow stripes on the blue-grey body of the car.

Jim got out of Herbie slowly, also feeling shaken up and worried that he was in for a fight.

'Easy now . . . I'm real sorry, buddy.'

'What do you mean – buddy!?'

The driver ripped off helmet and goggles to reveal – none other than Diane Darcy.

Jim was stunned – to put it mildly.

'Uh,' he stumbled. 'Um, Miss Buddy? Mrs Buddy? Ms Buddy? Er, Diane?'

Diane was fighting all right. Fighting for words. 'You . . . you . . . ' The only ones that came to her mind were not those which a well-brought up racing driver would use in company. At least, not a well-dressed, well-brought-up driver like Diane Darcy. She hastily pushed back into the innermost recesses of her spick and span mind and stared at Jim in disgust.

'I'm terribly sorry. Again.'

'Come on! You think just because I'm a woman driver

38

you can get away with anything you please! Well, I'm not a little bird for your fun and games. I've had it with you clowns. Had it up to here!'

Diane put her hand to her smooth and pretty neck. It was, Jim allowed himself, a most attractive prospect.

'Look, Diane, honestly, I wasn't the clown. It was Herbie.'

She stared at Wheely as if he'd that second crawled out of the end of a sump pump. 'You're blaming your dizzy mechanic?'

'No, you don't understand. Herbie's the car.' Jim changed his tone, became warmer, smoother – like Diane's neck – 'You see, Herbie's more like a person. Now I know that sounds sort of funny . . . '

'Crazy, more like. Like the two of you – and especially you!' She jabbed an elegantly gloved finger at Jim and turned and stalked back to her Lancia. Jim watched her go with a mixture of annoyance and longing. It was so long since he'd seen such an attractive girl – and a driver to boot.

Well, not to boot.

That wasn't exactly what Jim had in mind.

In a short time an angry and bewildered race official was addressing the drivers of the two cars.

'What were you doing out there, Douglas?'

'Well, it's pretty hard to explain, sir . . . '

'Not for me it isn't,' Diane interrupted. 'He doesn't want a woman in the race.'

The official did his best to calm things down. 'Look, Miss Darcy,' he said with a movement of the hands that was obviously meant to calm troubled waters. 'You'll be given another chance to qualify. We're terribly sorry . . . '

'You're sorry! He's sorry! Everybody's sorry! But the fact remains that I didn't qualify.'

She turned her back on the three men and strode back to her car, a very annoyed and disappointed young woman.

Jim looked at her going, unhappily. But there was no time for such emotions.

'As for you, Douglas, if you intend to qualify, you are due at the starting line. Now!'

Wheely leaned over Herbie and whispered. 'Hear that, pal? Forget that powder puff of a Lancia and get your mind on to the racing.'

There were eight cars lined up at the start, including those of Bruno and Gilbert – who had a space between them into which Herbie slid.

'Hey, Gilbert!' called Bruno with the ever-present smirk on his face. 'Look who comes between us – the cheese for the middle of the sandwich.'

The two European drivers exchanged meaningful winks as though they had arranged something for Herbie while waiting. And it wasn't going to be an invitation to a celebration afterwards. Not even a cheese sandwich!

The drivers revved up their engines and seconds later the starter dropped his flag to signal the start of the race.

Right from the start, the two cars on either side of Herbie raced off just ahead of him, then started to squeeze together so that it was impossible for Herbie to get through.

Jim did his best, but had to scowl and pull back, so letting his main rivals get ahead. Yards further on he made a fresh attempt to get past Bruno's number 17. But the German swung the red car with yellow and black markings right into Herbie, nicking his front wing.

Travelling at that speed, a bump like that was enough to send Herbie off course. Jim used all of the skill he could muster but he wasn't able to keep the car on the track.

Herbie spun off it and swung round in a cloud of dust. He was pointing in the wrong direction with Jim and Wheely peering through the dusty windscreen, looking for the other drivers.

'Where'd they go?' asked Wheely.

Jim pointed behind them. 'They went that-away. Man, I really got suckered by that Bruno. My driving's even rustier than I thought.'

Angry with himself, as well as with the German, Jim turned the steering wheel hard and brought Herbie back on to the track. As the little car picked up speed, he began to pass the back markers in the race, and then to get in sight of the leaders. Soon he was in third place, with only Gilbert and Bruno in front of him. Gilbert tried to stop Herbie from passing by weaving from side to side, but Jim finally managed to shoot inside him on a wide bend and leave him more or less stationary.

Now there was only Bruno to catch – and pass.

The two cars were drawn together as if by a magnet. Closer and closer and closer. Bruno's face could be seen in the mirror, his smile plastered on to his face like so much cheap wall paper.

'Better close your mouth, turkey,' shouted Wheely above the whine and roar of the engines. ' 'Cause you're going to get our tyre marks all over your teeth!'

Jim gritted his own teeth and began to make his move. The two cars were bumper to bumper on a straight stretch of the course and Herbie seemed to have the greater power.

He would pass him!

He would! He would!

Jim's face showed determination; Wheely's anticipation; for the first time Bruno's smirk seemed in danger of disintegration.

And then ...

And then ...

Along came the Lancia!

Diane Darcy's car was travelling along a road that overlooked that section of the course. Herbie had detected its presence somehow. And as soon as he looked up and saw her. Well!

The wheel wrenched to the right despite Jim's astonished efforts to stop it, and the next thing he knew Herbie was heading off the track.

'Hey, Herbie! What are you doin'?'

'It's her again.'

Herbie dashed up a dirt track towards the road along which the Lancia was travelling. A hundred yards further and a gate barred the way. There was no getting through; neither was there any getting round due to the spectators who lined the track. The Lancia disappeared into the distance and it was almost possible to hear Herbie's heart sink.

It was possible, however, to hear the same thing happen to Jim and Wheely. There was no chance now of them winning the first qualifying round.

CHAPTER THREE

Back at the Champs Elysées something stirred. Quincey, his cap and dirty raincoat making him as inconspicuous as a refrigerator in the middle of the Sahara, threaded his bulky way through the crowd that had gathered inside the motor showroom.

It was a large room freshly painted blue with red and blue strips of material dangling from it. A huge banner advertising the Trans-France race hung over the centre of the space.

A number of the more interesting cars entered for the race were on display and Herbie was supposed to be one of them. As far as Quincey was concerned, he had better be.

As Quincey slid between two of the crowd, a hand descended on to his shoulder.

Quincey nearly jumped through the ceiling. 'What the ... ?'

'Ssh!'

It was Max.

'Don't ever do that. It reminds me of ... '

'All right, we don't want to go into your criminal past.'

'Right. It's my criminal present I'm worried about. Did you see ... ' He lowered his voice. 'Double X?'

Max nodded. 'He wasn't happy.'

'Who is? And I can't find that dumb little car!'

'Patience. Let's ask someone.'

Max went off and looked for the man who had been the MC at the earlier meeting by the museum. 'Excuse me, sir. Some very impressive cars here. Uh, but I don't see the little Volkswagen . . . '

'Ah, you mean the Douglas car. Oh, it'll be here. Patience.'

Quincey glowered as the man walked off. 'If I hear another person say patience . . . '

'Well, you'd better have it now, because if we don't show up with that diamond, Double X is going to mark the spot where we get buried with two very large Xs.'

But the worried expression was drifting off Quincey's face. 'Don't start digging our graves yet. Look over there.'

Jim drove Herbie into the showroom with Wheely sitting beside him and most of the crowd turned to look at the new arrival. None of them were as pleased to see Herbie as the two thieves.

Quincey got hold of Max's arm. 'Come on! Let's grab it. And don't tell me "patience".'

'Sure,' said Max sarcastically. 'We'll go over there and get it back in front of a hundred people. All we have to do, after all, is to unscrew the petrol cap and plunge an arm down into the tank and pull out a diamond. Simple! Easy! No reason why anyone should think it even a little strange or try to stop us.'

'Okay, cleverdick, what do you suggest?'

'I suggest,' said Max, pulling at his waistcoat, 'that we need a plan.'

And at that moment – just like in all the best stories – a plan was presented right to them. The MC's voice came over the loudspeaker announcing that it was time for a film of the route to be shown.

Now, films are normally shown in the dark which meant that Max and Quincey could get up to their dirty work without being seen.

'I think,' announced Max, with a certain amount of glee, 'someone has made us a plan.'

The attendants began to draw the long curtains over the showroom windows. As they did so, Max glanced out through the narrowing gap and saw a Lancia drive slowly by in the street outside. He thought nothing of it – why should he?

Indeed, had he been the only person to notice the car's trim lines, it would not have mattered to the story at all.

But someone else spotted the Lancia – and that someone was Herbie!

The Volkswagen stared, did a double take, gasped and began to quiver all over.

The curtains were fully drawn shut. The lights were out. The majority of the crowd got into position to watch the screen. Only Max and Quincey moved in another direction; towards Herbie.

As the two men slowly backed through the crowd of spectators, little did they realise that Herbie was doing some backing away of his own. Away from the showroom and down the darkened corridor that led into the garage area beyond.

The narrator continued to tell the crowd about the beauties and dangers of the race route; Max and Quincey continued on their crafty way towards their objective.

Towards the most expensive petrol tank in the world.

Towards . . .

Quincey sensed something behind him and reached stealthily backwards, fingers of his hand extended. Opening. Grasping tight.

'I got something!' he hissed.

'You ab by dose, b'sur!' was hissed back at him through the darkness.

Quincey jumped but held on tight. What on earth?

Max, however, was well trained in languages – after reading for a degree in Swedish at Hull (he found the Swedish easier to understand than the local Hull dialect), he had mastered Swahili, Serbo-Croat and speaking-with-two-fingers-blocking-the-nasal-passages.

'He means,' said Max quietly, bending towards Quincey, 'that you have his nose – Monsieur.'

Quincey stared at Max – difficult in the almost total absence of light – shuffled his fingers around a little, became convinced his friend was right and quickly withdrew them.

'I don't think we've got back far enough,' said Quincey, wiping his fingers on his raincoat.

'Quite.'

But however far they retreated, even to the back wall itself, they could find no sign of the little car. There were not even any more noses to pinch. And they could tell that the film was nearing an end as the narrator was coming to a climax in his commentary.

'Quick,' said Max, 'the car must be over this side. Let's find it before it's too late.'

'Right!'

And off they went. Never seeing the three pedestals which held the three trophies for those first home in the Trans-France Race.

'And for someone,' said the commentator, with a triumphant note, 'victory is just a step away.'

Exactly on cue, both Quincey and Max took that giant step. There was an almighty crash and they found themselves toppling over in the midst of a roaring and banging of pedestals and prizes.

The lights went on; everyone turned round; a cry of

amazement went up. Max and Quincey cowered underneath the debris, both trying to look apologetic instead of plain angry.

It was a few moments after the accident that Jim and Wheely realised something else was not quite right. They gazed around the showroom and ...

'Herbie!' Jim shouted.

Wheely shook his head. 'You mean no Herbie!'

They both hurried from the showroom, leaving Max and Quincey making their excuses to a horde of showroom officials.

On the Avenue George Fifth, the Lancia had been parked directly in front of a small sidewalk café. Couples sat chatting and enjoying the peaceful atmosphere and the Paris sunshine. Waiters moved between the tables in white coats and aprons, carrying drinks on little metal trays.

Herbie roared along the avenue, trying desperately to catch up with the Lancia. He was so anxious and travelling so fast that he almost missed his chance. Herbie was fifty yards past the café before he realised that she was outside.

There was a screech of brakes that made several heads turn in his direction. Herbie pulled up, quivering, and peered backwards through his rear lights. Yes, there she was!

Cautiously he started to back towards the Lancia.

Now that he was so close, he wasn't going to frighten the love of his life away. Even a splash caused by a passing lorry failed to deter Herbie in his quest.

If knights in armour could face dragons and witch-like women with snakes in their hair who turned men into tone, what was a little Parisian mud?

Rien, thought Herbie, who'd picked up a smattering of French.

Herbie revved his engine, shot his aerial up and down half a dozen times, then worked his windscreen wipers and water jets. All to no avail. No response whatsoever. The Lancia's eyelids remained firmly closed.

Herbie tried one of his special wolf whistles on his horn, but the only reaction was from one of the waiters in the café, who was startled enough almost to lose his grip on the tray.

Herbie was beginning to feel discouraged.

One more try. The whistle succeeded in disturbing the waiter even more and . . . yes, the Lancia's lids lifted half way, only to drop slowly down again.

Herbie couldn't understand it. Now she had seen who he was, why the strange reaction? Surely she hadn't forgotten him?

Then it slowly dawned on Herbie what the trouble was – the soaking of mud he had received from that passing lorry had covered up too much of his bodywork to make him distinguishable from any other Volkswagen.

All right, he thought, there's no use waiting here for the rain to come and wash me clean. Time to take matters into my own hands!

Herbie engaged gear and roared off down the avenue, looking for somewhere to restore his usual sparkling appearance.

There at the crossroads was a fountain. A beautiful circular fountain in the middle of an area of grass and flowers with boulevards stretching away from it on four sides.

Herbie rammed his way up over the pavement and on to the grass. He drove round and round, making sure that the falling water went over every part of his bodywork. Minutes later, when he drove off, Herbie was restored to all of his former glory.

He drove along one of the boulevards, then turned into a narrow cobbled street with parasols outside cafés and geraniums and other flowers in brightly painted tubs.

The street was so narrow that Herbie could only just squeeze along it without touching the things on either side.

Ah! An idea flashed through his carburettor to his brain. He veered to the right and collected a bunch of flowers in his rear fender.

No gentleman should go a-calling without a suitable tribute to the lady's beauty!

When the waiter saw the driverless car return with his bouquet he was about to pour wine into a customer's glass. The poor man was so distracted that it went on to the table cloth, into his own shoe, over his customer's smoothly brushed hair . . . everywhere but in the glass.

The customer was not pleased!

The waiter wasn't exactly overjoyed either.

But the Lancia . . . !

Her eyelids opened and blinked fast; then they stayed open wide. It wasn't every day a handsome fellow brought her flowers – every other day, perhaps. But here in Paris . . . well, the Lancia was beginning to become infected by the romantic atmosphere of the city as well.

So it was that when Herbie drove slowly away along the Avenue George Fifth, the Lancia started her engine and gracefully pulled out and followed him.

It was more than the waiter could cope with. One car without a driver was bad enough. But two! It was more than one man could take. And to announce to the world his failure to deal with it, the waiter threw his tray of glasses into the air and sprawled forwards across one of the tables in a faint.

Oh, Herbie, see the trouble your love has caused! But then, I hear your murmur, what about Romeo and Juliet, Kermit the Frog and Miss Piggy?

The course of true love, when did it ever run smooth? Especially for an ageing Volkswagen and a scintillating Lancia!

Only a short while after the two cars had disappeared into the romantic distance, Diane Darcy came out of the café. She walked briskly and smartly towards the pavement, looking so attractive that most male heads turned in her direction.

She was wearing a striped blazer, coloured red, white and blue, over a blue skirt. Underneath the blazer was a contrasting blue blouse, with a blue and white scarf tied at her neck. The whole outfit was set off by a silver necklace that sparkled in the sunlight as she moved.

Such a beautiful woman in a city with more beautiful women to the square yard than any other!

Such a delicate, ladylike...

'My car!' Diane screamed in a voice guaranteed to send ships back into harbour in a force eight gale. 'Where's my car?! It was parked right out there!'

She stormed back into the café and picked up the nearest waiter, who was drooping over a table coming out of his faint.

'My car!' shouted Diane.

'*Mon dieu!*' called the waiter and proceeded to faint again.

But Diane was anything but bashful and kind heart never won over faint waiter. She picked up a carafe of water and threw it over him.

He blubbered his way back to consciousness and shook his head, sending sprays of water in all directions.

51

'My car. It was parked just outside.'

'The ... the little blue and yellow one?'

'Yes. It's gone.'

'Ah, yes,' agreed the waiter, wide-eyed and almost legless, 'it is gone.'

'Well, did you see who took it?'

'Not exactly, M'mselle ...'

'Oh, really! This is too stupid for words. I bet anything that some one connected with the race has stolen my car to prevent me from winning.'

At which point, Jim and Wheely ran into sight round the corner.

'You!' called Diane, moving towards them. 'I should have known I'd see you. You and trouble go together.'

But Jim was too worried to take Diane seriously. 'Look, we haven't got time for that. We're missing our car. You haven't seen it, have you?'

Diane made a face: not a particularly nice one. 'Who cares about your silly little Volkswagen. My Lancia has been stolen.'

The waiter held on to the nearest table for support. 'Your ... your ... but I saw them both.'

'You did!' Three voices echoed.

'*Oui, oui, oui.*'

'What happened?' they all asked him in chorus.

'You will not believe this, but ...'

'Go on!'

'It sounds too silly for words ...'

'Go on! Go on!'

'But it does not make any kind of sense at all ...'

'Go on! Go on! Go on!'

The waiter put his hands over his face, peering through the fingers of one hand and speaking through the other. 'No one will believe this, but I think one of the cars was trying to steal the other.'

'You mean?' three voices sang out.

'*Oui*, they were stealing away together!'

Jim and Wheely exchanged a quick look, realising what had happened. Jim grabbed Diane by the arm.

'Come on!'

They ran along the pavement, Jim frantically signalling for a taxi.

The waiter, still shaking his head, watched them go. Then he staggered back into the tables at the front of the café and reached for the nearest full bottle.

A suave customer looked up, startled, as his wine was taken from his hand. He was even more surprised to see the waiter put the bottle to his lips and swig it down in long gulps.

Diane, Jim and Wheely had found a taxi and were beginning a desperate search for their runaways. It was not going to be easy in a city the size of Paris.

Half an hour later all they had achieved was running up a big bill on the meter. Of Herbie and the Lancia they had seen nothing. Three false alarms had been the best they could manage.

'Talk about a needle in a haystack,' said Wheely. 'How are we ever gonna find them?'

'Search me,' said Jim.

It didn't seem the best of ideas: there was simply nowhere on his person large enough for two cars to hide.

'Look,' said Diane, getting increasingly worried, 'my life is riding on that car.'

'Lady, I've got a couple of things to prove myself.'

The taxi continued its tour of the Paris streets; three faces continued to peer out of the window, looking more and more forlorn.

Then Jim had an idea. It may have taken a long time

coming, but an idea it was. He recognised it from several he'd had some time before.

'Look, Diane,' he said, leaning towards her, 'where would you like to be taken by a guy on your first trip to Paris?'

The slap didn't hurt too much; considering that she was a girl with a strong right arm.

'Hey, watch that!'

'Well, what do you expect? Making passes at a time like this!'

'That wasn't a pass.'

'You could have fooled me.'

'That's not too difficult,' mumbled Wheely.

'Lady,' said Jim, 'when I make a pass there won't be any mistaking what it is. That was an idea as to where we might find your precious Lancia.'

'And your . . . your stupid Herbie.'

For a moment it seemed as if Wheely was going to biff her one back, but Jim restrained him. 'Listen, if I had romance in mind, would I have brought Wheely here along? The one who's made the pass is Herbie.'

'Herbie!'

'Sure. When you've known Herbie as long as we have, you know he's capable of anything.'

'More or less anything,' interrupted Wheely.

'Yes, sure. More or less.'

'I still can't believe it.'

'Okay, suit yourself, but it's worth a try isn't it?'

Diane shrugged her pretty shoulders. 'I suppose so.'

'Good. So where would you like to get taken on your first date in Paris?'

'I suppose something like a boat trip along the Seine would be . . . '

Jim called out to the driver. 'Take us to the Seine, right away!'

The driver turned towards them with a smile on his face. '*Oui*, Monsieur, certainly. You are not the only visitors to Paris today who want to see the river. I have just heard on the radio, two cars have taken a ride along it on a boat.'

'On a boat! Get there as fast as you can.'

'*Oui*, Monsieur. The Pont de l'Alma, right away.'

It took them less than five minutes to get to the bridge. Less than five seconds to spot the boat, which was travelling through at the same time as they arrived. And there on the deck, front wheels over the edge and taking in the view, were Herbie and the Lancia.

Diane looked round, confused.

'Maybe I could explain over dinner tonight?'

Her expression changed rapidly to a glare.

'Maybe not.'

But Jim wasn't too disheartened. He had found Herbie again and tomorrow he was to have another crack at qualifying for the big race. Diane would wait. Happily.

CHAPTER FOUR

While the search for Herbie and his young 'lady' had been going on, a quite different scene had been played out in a small Paris hotel room. Max stood almost to attention, wearing a beige suit and an expression which suggested that he was far from enjoying what he was doing. Which was speaking into the telephone.

'We were just backing up to the gas tank, sir, then the next thing the car just disappeared. Uh, yes, sir . . . we did come to you highly recommended . . . yes, because we are highly efficient. I guarantee we'll get it this time. We got the hotel staked out. As soon as it's dark, we'll grab the diamond.'

Max stopped talking and listened: he listened very carefully. From the far side of the room, Quincey was getting more and more frightened with every word. And he couldn't hear what was being said.

'Oh yes, sir,' replied Max finally, his face drained of any shade of colour. 'I understand.'

Max replaced the phone on the hook and stood there for several moments, the material of his suit trembling as if in a heavy wind.

'Guess he's pretty mad, huh?' Quincey ventured.

'Oh, no. He just said that the next time the car disappears, *we* disappear!'

In another room of the same hotel, Jim and Wheely were discussing what had happened with Herbie and their plans for the coming day. Wheely had that moment returned from giving the car its final going over.

'All taken care of, Jim. Had a little straight talk with Herbie.'

'Hum, I wonder if that will be enough?'

'What do you mean?'

Jim got up from the easy chair and handed Wheely a newspaper. 'Take a look at this.'

Wheely opened out the paper. There was a picture of Herbie plastered right across the front page and above it a caption that read something Wheely failed to understand. Jim translated it for him: CAN CRAZY CAR COME BACK?

'Come on, Jim, you don't take that seriously, do you. I mean . . .'

'Twelve years is a long time. The pressure's really on. I sure hope we can handle it. And when I say "we", that means all of us. You. Me. And that . . . that "crazy car".'

'Don't talk that way, Jim. I've told you. I spoke to Herbie – sort of man to man, well, man to car. I told him I don't mind having a car that's got a heart, but there's one thing I won't tolerate and that's a car falling in love with another car.'

Jim took back the newspaper and slapped it against his leg. 'What d'you want him to do? Fall in love with the Goodyear Blimp?'

'I told him, "Herbie, we're over here for one thing and one thing only . . . to make the biggest comeback in racing history. No women in training camp! You got to forget this chick! You can do it. It's just a matter of mind over metal!" '

Jim was still looking doubtful. His expression changed to surprise when there was a knock on the door; a knock that sounded official.

Wheely opened the door to reveal Inspector Bouchet and his assistant, Detective Fontenoy. The young detective stepped forward briskly. 'Detective Fontenoy here. And this . . . this is the famous Inspector Bouchet.'

Jim offered his hand to the Inspector. 'I'm Jim Douglas. This is my partner, Wheely Applegate.'

The four men exchanged greetings and sat down, the room looking smaller with all of them in it.

'Look,' Wheely began, 'if it's about that car of ours riding down the river on the boat, well . . . '

The Inspector raised a hand. 'Boat? River? No, no. This is something far more important.' He sat forward in his chair and lowered his voice. 'It's a matter concerning the six-million-dollar diamond that was stolen this morning.'

Jim and Wheely looked at one another and for no reason felt the finger of guilt creep over them.

The Inspector shrewdly grasped this and tried to set them at their ease. 'It is simply that we are questioning everyone who was in the area at the time. Perhaps you can help us . . . '

Jim and Wheely looked at one another again and sat back, feeling more relaxed. Here was a man they could trust . . .

Outside were the two men about whom they would have felt exactly the opposite – had they been able to see them. Max and Quincey moved cautiously along by the hotel wall, looking past the line of cars that was parked there leading up to the hotel.

Yes, there it was! The little Volkswagen they were seeking.

They dropped back into the shadows of the quiet street, then eased their way forward again, making certain that no one could see them.

A couple strolled by arm in arm and the two erstwhile thieves disappeared into the darkness, emerging moments later as the sound of footsteps faded away.

Max sidled up to Herbie's petrol tank and tried to unfasten the cap. It refused to budge and as he wrestled with it, Herbie lurched suddenly forward.

Max looked round at Quincey in desperation.

'Pushing the car won't help.'

'I didn't push it. It must have rolled.'

'Then get inside and pull on the brake while I get this off.'

Quincey tried both door handles and then the windows, but it was no good.

'I thought you could get into any car made?'

'I can!'

Quincey tried one of the side windows again and smiled. His hand slipped inside and began to reach forward. As they did so, Herbie closed the window sharply on Quincey's prying fingers.

'Ooowww!'

'For heaven's sake, keep quiet! You want the police round here or something?'

Quincey wasn't saying. He was too busy hopping about on the pavement like a man wanting to break the all-European hopscotch record.

'Give me a hand over here then.'

Quincey offered his bruised fingers. 'Here. Have this one. It isn't a lot of use to me at the moment.'

The two of them were getting desperate. They pounded Herbie's hood with their fists and angrily kicked at the tyres. But nothing they did got them any closer to their goal.

'Right,' said Max. 'I'm hot-wiring this car. We'll take it to the garage and get the diamond out there.'

While Max headed for the rear of the car, Quincey picked up a nearby sign with a concrete bottom and advanced on Herbie with it.

'I'm warning you, car. It's me or you!'

He raised the sign above his head and threatened to slam it down on Herbie's roof. Herbie whipped his door open and smashed it into Quincey's stomach. Quincey dropped the sign and staggered backwards in surprise and pain.

'Uuuh! Ooowww!'

'For the last time,' hissed Max, 'will you shut up?'

Quincey did so by falling over and knocking the breath out of his body. Max lifted Herbie's rear hood and tried to find the right wire to get the engine started. But Herbie didn't like strangers fiddling about with his insides.

In protest, he started up and blasted a thick stream of black smoke out of his exhaust, blinding Max, who staggered backwards and tripped over the edge of the kerb.

Two down and one to go – that one being Herbie.

He pulled away from the kerb and drove away quickly up the street. Max and Quincey sat up and stared after the disappearing car in amazement.

'I suppose,' said Quincey, 'you're going to tell me that that car just started up and drove off by itself?'

Max was still rubbing his eyes. 'No . . . and I'm not going to tell it to Double X either. Come on!'

They clambered to their feet and started to run off in the direction that Herbie had taken.

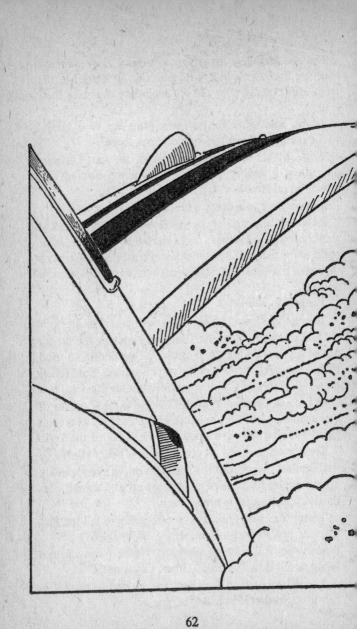

Herbie had lost his pursuers and got back to the hotel in time for a good rest. He didn't want to let Jim and Wheely down the next day – or himself.

So with a large and interested crowd clamouring round, Herbie was pushed to the starting line of the last two qualifying heats the next day.

'Ladies and gentlemen,' said the announcer, 'the first three places only will qualify for a place in the Trans-France Race.'

Bruno sauntered up to Jim and Wheely with his usual smug expression firmly in place. 'The others, Douglas, get to go home early. So *bon voyage*.'

Wheely snarled at Bruno's back as he walked cockily away. 'We'll be going home as soon as we collect that trophy from Monte Carlo.'

'Somehow,' said Jim quietly, 'I'm not as confident as you are.'

'You wait and see. After that lecture I gave him last night, there's going to be a new Herbie out there today.'

Jim said nothing, simply hoping his partner was right. Now it was a matter of doing as well behind the wheel as he could and hoping that Herbie would respond.

Soon they were off amidst the smell of burning rubber and a flurry of dust. When the cars came out of the first turn Herbie was not among the leaders.

Wheely peered out through the windscreen, trying to see through the trails of exhaust smoke. 'Where are we?'

'Well,' said Jim bitterly, 'since there are eight cars ahead of us, that puts us last.'

Jim had his foot on the floor on the straight, but Herbie seemed hardly to be moving.

'A new Herbie!? He isn't even an old Herbie. He isn't any Herbie at all.'

'My whole lecture must have fallen on a deaf carburettor.'

'He doesn't need a lecture, he needs an old age pension. I think he's all through. Now listen, Herbie, and listen good! You and I didn't come out of mothballs to be the laughing stock of the continent. Now if you don't get the lead out of your pants right now, I'm going to have you stuffed and shipped back to the States and hung on the wall in Retirement Village.'

Jim thought his angry speech had been wasted, when as if magically Herbie's engine took on a new note of defiance and the car powered forward.

'Now you're talking. Is this the old Herbie?'

'That's the old and the new Herbie rolled into one!'

The car zipped past three of the back markers and zoomed into a bend so fast that it seemed to go round it on no more than two wheels.

'If he wouldn't do it for you,' said Jim to Wheely, 'it looks as if he's doing it for me.'

'Oh, no. He isn't doing it for either of us. He's doing it for *her*!'

Wheely pointed towards the stands, where Diane Darcy was standing watching, waiting to go in the second race. And there close to the edge of the stands was the Lancia, also pointed towards the race track and watching.

Herbie put on even more speed as they passed the Lancia for the second time and went into the final lap with only two cars to catch. They screeched past one half way round and came level with the leader when the stands were once more in sight.

'Go on, Herbie! You can do it!' Jim shouted as he held tight to the wheel.

'Course he can.'

And he did. Herbie took the leader as if he wasn't moving at all and came level with the stands. He moved over towards the Lancia and stunned Jim and Wheely – and the crowd – by doing a full turn in the centre of the track. His bow to the Lancia made and his masculinity proved by defeating all rivals, Herbie satisfied himself by crossing the line a clear winner.

The officials checked their watches, puzzled at the time they had recorded. Could it be true? A crowd of excited spectators hurried towards the car and a race official pushed his way through them.

'Amazing! Quite amazing! A new record for this track. You have shattered Von Stickle's time!'

'Congratulations, Douglas,' said Gilbert with a scowl. 'You have just won the right to taste my dust tomorrow.'

'And mine,' said Bruno. 'You may have broken my record here, Douglas, but tomorrow it should be a different matter. I will turn your "hello comeback" into a "goodbye forever".'

And the rival drivers stalked off, planning how to do Herbie down.

Jim climbed out of the car, his orange driving suit streaked with sweat.

'Come on,' said Wheely, 'it's Diane's race now. At least we've got to give Herbie a chance to see his lady friend performing. He's earned that all right.'

Diane was wearing a new white driving suit and a look of determination that ensured she would do well. What added the extra vitamins to the Lancia's performance, though, was Herbie's presence on the rails.

The sleek car outdid itself in a powerful display of speed that exceeded Diane's expectations and took her round the track in the lead almost from start to finish.

It was the second amazing result of the day.

The race official dashed up to Diane as she was getting out of the car in the pits and told her as much.

Diane flushed with pleasure: 'Yes. I knew I had a good car under me, but . . .'

'What is more, it was the exact same time as the

Douglas car. And equal track record.'

'Congratulations,' said Jim, walking up from the other side of the pits.

'Thank you,' replied Diane. But she wasn't being very gracious. Nor friendly. 'And thank you for staying off the track this time. That's one way I can prove what I can do.'

'Well,' said Jim with a half-smile, 'it wasn't exactly your doing you know. Not all of it.'

Diane stood with her hands firmly on her hips. 'You've really got a problem about women in racing, Mr Douglas. What is it? Do we drive too slow for your liking? Or should that be too fast?'

'That's not what I meant. It isn't you or I at all. It's that car of yours . . . and my car.'

Diane threw up her hands in a sign of disgust and began to walk away. Jim started to go after her.

'Excuse me,' she snapped over her shoulder. 'I don't want to hear about your car again.'

Jim caught hold of her arm and stopped her in her tracks. 'Wait! Herbie's not just a car. Would you believe me if I told you that he's got a . . . uh . . . that he can really . . . uh . . . ' Jim ran out of words and touched his heart. 'I didn't believe it myself at first. But when a car like Herbie with a . . . uh . . . well, when a car like Herbie who's got what he's got comes to Paris and meets a beautiful Lancia who's also got a . . . uh . . . also got the same as he's got. Well, then you can't blame them for falling in . . . uh . . . uh . . . '

Diane was simply standing there staring at Jim as he stuttered to a halt like an old-fashioned train running out of steam.

Jim realised he was getting nowhere in convincing her. 'You're right. I wouldn't believe it either if I were you.'

Diane backed away. 'When the men come from the Booby Hatch, go quietly.'

'I was just trying to warn you about your car.'

Diane had just about had enough. She lashed round with an arm and pointed at Jim as though he were on the verge of attacking her. There was an expression of fierce anger on her face that made such a thought – not that it had been in Jim's mind at all – a very foolish one.

'Well, let me warn you about *me*! I'm in this race to *win*! And frankly, there's nothing I'd like more than to see you and that stupid car of yours disappear entirely!'

With that she stalked off, leaving Jim looking like a man who'd lost a pound note and found a penny.

'A charm school,' muttered Wheely who'd been watching from a safe distance, 'would work wonders round here.'

Later in the day Jim and Wheely were driving Herbie back from the track, which was situated out in the country, towards Paris. Neither of them were looking as happy as they should have been, considering they'd clocked record time and won equal first position on the starting grid for the race proper.

'Having that Diane and her car in the race might be a problem,' said Wheely.

'She is a pretty good driver.'

'It's not the girl driver I'm worried about – it's the girl car. How d'you think Herbie's going to do with his girl friend in the race?'

It was a problem.

And there was another. Jim and Wheely weren't aware of it yet, but they were about to. As they drove past a grove of trees to the right of the road a large black sedan whipped out of hiding and set off after them. Nor was the car trying to follow from a distance and keep out of sight. He was moving up close – and fast.

'What are those clowns up to?' asked Jim, glancing at the rear view mirror.

He was soon about to find out. Max was behind the wheel and Quincey was sitting next to him. Max brought the sedan up parallel, trying to force Herbie off the road.

'Yeah!' said Wheely nervously, 'what are they trying to do?'

The sedan smacked into Herbie and sent him jolting sideways.

'Hey – watch it!' Jim yelled across.

The black sedan banged into them a second time and Jim had to fight to keep Herbie on the road at all.

'I'll tell you what they're trying to do. They're trying to kill us!'

Max brought the car over again and Quincey stuck a pistol out of the window. 'Pull over!' he ordered. 'We want that car!'

'What are you going to do?' asked Wheely, obviously frightened.

'Pull over.'

Jim slowed Herbie down and stopped the car by the verge. The sedan stopped right behind and Max and Quincey started to get out. At that moment Herbie's steering wheel spun itself sideways and the little car swung off the verge and down an embankment at the side of the roadway.

'Herbie! Herbie?'

But there was no stopping him now. Jim and Wheely might have been willing to give in at the sight of a gun, but not Herbie. He was made out of stronger stuff – or should that be sterner metal?

Max and Quincey scrambled back into their car and gave chase. Herbie led them a merry one. He went through a gypsy camp full of wagons and trailers, tents, lines packed with colourful washing, zig-zagging between

obstacles. The sedan was too large to make the same manoeuvres. Soon it was skidding to a halt underneath a welter of awnings and washing and tents. Gypsies advanced on Max and Quincey looking not at all pleased with the interruption.

'Get us out of here!' shouted Quincey.

'I can't see a thing!'

'I don't care. Get going!'

With an awning right over the windscreen, the sedan reversed as quickly as Max could manage it.

Meanwhile, Herbie had come across a number of gypsies having a picnic. A long trestle table led to a spit upon which a pig was being roasted. There seemed no way in which Herbie could avoid smashing into the whole scene.

'Yeoowww!' screamed Wheely, putting both hands over his eyes.

Jim held his breath.

Herbie gave a mighty effort and roared up on to the end of the table and raced along it, using it for a ramp for a flying take-off that launched the little car high into the air, clearing the fire and the roasting pig.

The sedan, once again, was more cumbersome. It wrecked the table and drove right through the middle of the fire sending the pig high into the air.

High . . . high . . . higher . . . then down like a bomb, right through the top of the car!

Max looked sideways; Quincey looked sideways. The pig was sitting in the front seat between them, an apple still in his mouth. Not that a little thing like a pig was going to come between them and their quest. They saw Herbie at the far side of the field and set off after him.

Wheely looked back nervously and saw the sedan careering dangerously towards them.

'They're still coming.'

Jim nodded grimly. 'I think they *are* trying to kill us.'

Herbie swung out of the field on to a road under construction. Ahead was a huge sewer pipe that was being laid into the ground. The workmen looked up in alarm as the little Volkswagen bore down on them. They dropped their picks and shovels and scattered as Herbie headed directly for the end of the pipe, and gasped as he shot into it and disappeared.

The three workmen who had been inside the pipe came rushing out at the far end, closely followed by Herbie. As the little car made its escape there was an enormous rending crash and crunch from the front end.

The sedan had been a little too ambitious again. Like the ex-athlete who thinks he can still leap the hurdles and falls and breaks his leg, Max dreamed of being the young driver of a slim sports car.

The results of middle-aged fantasy were ever thus!

The front half of the sedan was jammed into the end of the pipe, with the metal pushed back to the side of the doors. The men in the front were still vibrating with the impact of the collision – to say nothing of the pig.

Only now the apple was in Quincey's mouth instead. It had been a long time since he'd been rendered speechless – but then, he was shaken to the core!

He peeled himself off the seat and gazed at the dust of Herbie's escape. When he did take the apple from his mouth, his language was fruity to say the least.

Herbie, realising the enemy had been lost for now, had slowed down.

'I didn't think she'd go that far to make us disappear.'

'Who's that?' asked Jim, puzzled.

'That cute little time-bomb, Diane. She set us up to knock us out of the race just like she said she would.'

'Wait a minute, she never said that.'

Wheely grinned. 'Of course not. They never say what

they mean. That's what makes the female of the species more deadly than the male.'

Jim looked at him doubtfully. 'You read that somewhere.'

'Well, I've had a mother, three sisters and two wives to prove it. They never told me they wanted me out of the house. But everytime I came home the lock had been changed.'

'Hmm, I don't take that kind of strong-arm stuff from anybody . . . male or female.'

'Then somebody had better teach this female the rules of the game . . . before it's over!'

Jim grew determined to do exactly that. 'I'll tell you what, Wheely, if she doesn't know now, she will when I get through with her!'

Wheely looked well pleased. He would like to be a fly on the wall when it came to that particular showdown!

As it happened, things were not to be as he imagined them.

Jim put on a new reddish-brown sweater and a smart yet casual blue denim jacket to visit Diane's hotel room. Diane herself was wearing a beige silk dress with maroon and blue patterns on it and a maroon scarf.

Two smart young people – maybe not quite so young in Jim's case – meeting by night in Paris. What could happen?

Slam!

A vase flew across the room and crashed into tiny pieces not far from Jim's head.

'*Me!* Me try to wreck your car??? Get out! *Out!*'

She pointed to the door and Jim hesitated. Diane stopped pointing and picked up an ash tray.

'Who hired thugs?! I don't have to hire anyone to win

74

my races for me! I'm as good as anyone on that track. Better!'

Jim opened his mouth to speak, but before he could . . .

'That's the trouble with you . . . all of you men. You don't think a woman can do anything! I've taken it all my life. Women are supposed to be nurses, secretaries . . . schoolteachers . . . things like that. I took it from my father, my mother, my aunts and uncles . . . but I'm not taking it any more. And especially not from you!'

Jim ducked down to avoid the ashtray that went soaring between them.

'Stand still, you coward! I'm a race driver and I can win on my own. Now do you understand that? I can win on my own!'

Jim ducked outside as something else crashed against the door and smashed to smithereens.

'You know,' he said to the woodwork, 'I think maybe you can.'

'Oh, boy,' sang out Wheely, when Jim climbed back into Herbie, 'I wish I could have been there. I bet you really told that chick what for! Yes, sir, I bet you really gave it to her straight. Oh, boy!'

Wheely went on for some time . . . but Jim was oddly, singularly silent.

'Tell me what you said to her, Jim. Tell me exactly what you told her to put her in her place. I know there's no holding you once you get going. Jim. Jim? Jim?'

Jim drove on into the darkness of the Paris night – in silence.

CHAPTER FIVE

Later that night Inspector Bouchet was having a very serious and intense conversation on the private telephone in his office. He listened for quite long periods, his mood changing from bad to worse as the conversation continued. Every now and then he interrupted with a terse remark that showed his displeasure even more.

'Don't tell me there has been another complication! As far as I can see, the only complication we are troubled with here is yourself!'

Pause.

'The item should have been in my hands by now.'

Pause. The Inspector drummed the desk top with his fingers.

'Imbeciles! I give you a perfect plan and what do you give me in return? Excuses!'

Pause. The Inspector chewed one of his finger nails.

'Impossible! How can it have disappeared? Again! Are you trying to tell me that a couple of simple-minded ...'

There was a further pause while the Inspector focused his attention through the glass panel and into the outer office where Jim and Wheely were arriving.

The Inspector hissed, 'Hold on!' into the phone and

put his hand over the receiver as the two Americans were shown into his office.

'I hope we're not disturbing you,' said Jim politely, unsure of how the great French policeman would treat their interruption.

But he did not seem bothered; not at all. 'No, no, gentlemen. Your timing could not have been more perfect. I want to thank you for your continued co-operation in this matter of the stolen diamond.'

'Well, Inspector, it's your help we're after now.'

'You see,' cut in Wheely, 'someone's out to get our car.'

The Inspector's face remained bland and unimpressed by the suggestion. 'But that seems impossible.'

'I think they're trying to knock us out of the race,' Jim explained. 'Is there some way we could have him out under protective custody for the night?'

The Inspector gulped in anticipation. 'Excuse me, gentlemen,' he said, quickly putting his hand to his mouth. 'I have a slight case of hiccups.'

'That is,' said Wheely, 'if you're not too busy trying to find the diamond.'

'No, no,' said the Inspector quickly. 'One is as important as the other, I assure you. Er, I'll only be a moment then we will attend to your problem.'

He pointed at the telephone still in his other hand.

'Oh, sure,' said Jim, 'maybe we'd better wait outside till you've finished.'

'Yes, make sure no one steals the car. We don't want anything to happen to it now.'

The Inspector waited for the two Americans to leave, then spoke quietly into the phone; 'Hello . . . the car is here. Never mind how. It is too risky for me to do what has to be done. I will see to it that the car will be at number 32 Avenue Picard within the hour. See you get there – and don't get lost on the way!'

The Inspector set down the telephone receiver and stood up, collected his overcoat and hat and left the station. Jim and Wheely were outside with Herbie.

'Your worry is now my worry, gentlemen. Rest easily. I'll take charge of this valuable property personally.'

He set his hand on the car door and was about to open it when a fresh voice came on the scene.

'Inspector...'

It was the ever-present, ever-keen, ever-trying Detective Fontenoy.

'What is it?' asked the Inspector, plainly annoyed.

'Off duty or not, sir, I could not help thinking about the diamond. And I knew that it must be preying on your mind too, stopping you from sleeping.'

'At the moment, Fontenoy,' the Inspector snarled, 'I've got a *car* weighing on *my* mind.'

'For some reason,' Jim explained, 'someone's been trying to knock us out of the race.'

'With your excellent time in the trials, it will not take a master of deduction like Inspector Bouchet to see that you have a fine chance of winning.'

Inspector Bouchet nodded aggressively. 'Which is why I personally will ensure the safety of this automobile. Now, put your minds at ease, gentlemen. Get a good night's sleep.'

Wheely patted Herbie fondly. 'That goes for you, too, Herbie.'

'Right,' said Jim, 'we've got a big day tomorrow.'

He and Wheely turned to go and the Inspector once more went to open the car door. Again Fontenoy stopped him.

'No, no. Permit me, sir.'

'Wh... what do you mean?'

'You have enough responsibility trying to locate the

diamond. I'll look after the car.'

'Don't be ridiculous!' Inspector Bouchet boomed.

Jim and Wheely started to walk away, surprised at the policeman's outburst. Bouchet nodded to them and gestured that everything was all right. But when he went back to the car, Fontenoy was climbing into the driving seat.

'Fontenoy! What are you doing?'

The young detective smiled: 'Anything for you and the force, Inspector.'

Bouchet leaned over to the window. 'Fontenoy. Get out of this car!'

But Fontenoy sat firm and the Inspector had to smile at the Americans again as they were looking a little confused at this lack of co-operation in the French police force.

'Fontenoy,' Bouchet hissed, 'you don't understand.'

Fontenoy smiled and nodded. 'That's all right, Inspector, even such a great man as you must show a little strain sometimes. Which is exactly why *I'll* take responsibility for this little car so that no one will find it.'

And, so saying, the detective drove off around the corner and out of sight.

Bouchet turned to Jim and Wheely with a shrug. 'My best man, Fontenoy.' He looked back at where the Volkswagen had been moments before and shook his head rather sadly. 'My very best.'

Hours later the dawn was beginning to break over the Paris rooftops and Inspector Bouchet was still in his darkened office. The telephone startled him out of near slumber.

'Yes? Yes? Oh! . . . Nowhere? . . . I have trained that Fontenoy too well, alas for me! . . . But tomorrow the car will have to refuel at the start of the race. When it does, we will be ready.'

Bouchet set down the phone and looked out of the window to the slowly spreading light. And because there was nothing else to do, he reached for his well-thumbed copy of Proust from his shelf and started to read, thinking that it would at least give him patience – or send him to sleep.

At the foot of the Eiffel Tower, banners had been put up advertising the official start of the Trans-France Race. Coloured balloons in large quantities were suspended above the starting area, ready to be released over the spectators. Temporary stands had been set up to hold a large crowd, which was getting more and more excited as the morning wore on and the cars made their appearances.

Each one drew a cheer from this or that section of the audience. But a large number of them was waiting for the little American Volkswagen to make its appearance – after all, they had been reading so much about it in the newspapers.

'Ladies and Gentlemen,' came the announcement. 'As you can see the moment we have been waiting for is almost upon us.'

Expectation grew. Tempers grew short. Faces showed tension. Words were few and meaningful. Minutes ticked by faster and faster. For Jim and Wheely, in the midst of all that pent-up excitement, there was only one thing wrong. One thing missing.

Herbie.

Inspector Bouchet hurried over towards the two Americans, looking almost as worried as they were themselves.

'Inspector,' said Jim, 'it's nearly race time and there's no sign of Herbie yet. Where is he?'

Bouchet shrugged. 'Believe me, I'm as concerned as

you are. But I'm sure Fontenoy will be here. He may be unpredictable, but he's dependable. Let me check with headquarters again.'

The Inspector walked off, stopping by a petrol lorry to talk to two men in 'Trans-France' overalls and sunglasses.

'Where is it?' asked one of them, bearing an uncanny resemblance to Max.

'Don't worry,' Bouchet muttered, 'it'll be here. You just be ready.' The Inspector walked away.

The second petrol attendant came forward, staring after the behatted figure of the Inspector in surprise. 'Who's that?' he asked in a voice not dissimilar from that of Quincey.

'That,' whispered Max knowingly, 'is none other than the mastermind.'

'Not ... ?' gasped Quincey.

'Yes. Double X.'

Quincey was so astonished he tripped over his own feet and fell headlong to the ground. Jim's first sight of Diane that morning had a similar effect. It wasn't that she was looking stunningly beautiful – which she undoubtedly was – but more that Jim thought she might be about to shy the shiny spanner she was holding in her gloved hand in his direction.

'Don't look so worried,' she said. 'I've calmed down now.'

Jim didn't look too certain. 'About last night,' he began unsurely.

Diane nodded: 'I'm sorry.'

'Not for missing me with that vase, I hope?'

'No, no,' she smiled. 'I was more than a little uptight, I guess. Probably nervous about the race.'

Jim made a face. 'I was kind of out of line myself. Too ready to throw blame ... in the wrong direction.'

Diane came a few paces closer, the spanner out of sight behind her back. 'We didn't get off to what you might call a flying start.'

'No,' Jim ventured with a smile. 'Herbie and I take a little getting used to.'

Diane stepped back again. 'When you include Herbie like that you really do take a lot of getting used to.' She paused and looked around. 'By the way. Where is . . . er, he?'

Bruno Von Stickle and Claude Gilbert were coming over with the same question in mind.

'Misplaced your little car, Douglas?' sneered Bruno.

'Just temporarily.'

'Turn over a rock or two,' suggested Gilbert sarcastically. 'You might find it there.'

'Not a rock, Gilbert,' said Bruno. 'You mean a gravestone.'

Any retort that Jim and Wheely might have made was cut off by a fresh announcement over the loudspeaker system.

'Attention, everyone. Would all drivers bring their machines to the grid. Five minutes till race time. Thank you.'

Jim and Wheely exchanged frustrated looks while Bruno and Gilbert could not have seemed more pleased if they'd already shared first prize.

'It's just as well, Douglas,' Bruno rubbed it in. 'You know the saying: "They never come back".'

Jim gritted his teeth as the two continental drivers strolled away towards their cars.

'I'd better go,' said Diane, looking rather sad.

Jim shook her hand: 'Good luck, anyway.'

'I think you mean that. Thanks.' And she hurried off to the Lancia.

Soon the cars were being pushed into position on the

boulevard, making eight rows of four abreast. There were two gaps at the front of the line – one for Herbie, the other for the Lancia. It was obvious that Diane couldn't get her car to start.

'Oh, no!' moaned Wheely. 'That Lancia's waiting for Herbie!'

Not only the Lancia. Jim and Wheely. Max and Quincey. Inspector Bouchet. The entire race.

'I hope you had nothing to do with this,' said Diane, hurrying over.

'No,' said Jim, 'but I think Wheely can get her started for you.'

Diane raised an eyebrow, but followed the two men back to her car nevertheless.

One of the mechanics offered Wheely his tools, but Wheely simply lifted the Lancia's hood and started to talk. 'Listen,' he said, 'I know how you feel, but you better get over it right now. Forget Herbie. You know why he's not here, don't you? He's found somebody else, that's why. He didn't have the guts to tell you himself, so I'm telling you.'

Jim leaned over the engine and joined in. 'He's right. So far we've had to tell this to a Fiat, a Thunderbird and an Austin-Healey. It was fun while it lasted. But the truth is, you weren't the first and you won't be the last. So take off!'

With Diane more sure than ever that Jim and Wheely were candidates for the nearest Funny Farm and the French mechanics scratching their heads and mumbling about these stupid Americans, the Lancia surprised them all by doing exactly that.

She took off.

Diane didn't understand how it had happened, but she wasn't about to argue. Not with the start of the race a minute away. She thanked the two Americans and climbed behind the steering wheel. With a blast from the exhaust she was away.

'Douglas,' called an official hurrying towards him, 'don't you realise you've got the pole position?'

'Sure. I also realise we don't at this precise moment have a car.'

'Well, Douglas, you have – what do you Americans say – blown it.'

Jim stood there, shaking his head in disgust at the sour taste that was forming in his mouth – he'd blown it all right. The taste of defeat.

The cars roared away in a thrill of sound and speed. The hundreds of balloons floated down over the crowd and one of them detached itself from the rest and slowly drifted down on to Jim's shoulder. From there it bounced lazily on to the ground by his feet and burst.

A sour taste indeed.

'Look! Look there!'

It was Wheely leaping about with sudden excitement. Jim looked in the direction he was pointing. He blinked and looked again. A large armoured truck was trundling towards them – and a familiar figure was in the driving cabin. Despite wearing a helmet and the uniform of an armed police guard, there was no mistaking the smiling, optimistic face of Fontenoy.

Better late than never!

The armoured truck swung slowly round so that the back was towards where Jim and Wheely were standing. Fontenoy jumped down from the cab and ran past the two astonished Americans to the back of the truck and started to open locks and loosen bolts.

He pulled back the door with a small shout of triumph and there was Herbie, sitting snugly inside.

'Great! Great!' said Wheely, 'but what took you so long?'

'Sorry. I would have been here sooner but I got held up.'

'You what?'

'Oh, no. Not that kind of hold-up. The traffic it was terrible. There was this policeman directing it and . . . ' He broke off when he saw the Inspector. 'Good morning, Inspector, how nice to see you on this beautiful morning . . . '

But Bouchet looked anything but happy with the morning. Jim and Wheely hurried off to check with the officials whether they could still join in the race.

'Certainly, Douglas, but it seems to me that you will be both starting and finishing last.'

Jim wasn't about to stand and argue. He would prove the man wrong in other ways. He and Wheely immediately started to push the car towards the petrol lorry – a fact which caused Bouchet to smile for the first time that morning. For instead of sending petrol into the tank, he knew that Max and Quincey were equipped to suck everything out.

Which meant the diamond. Which meant . . .

'Stop!' shouted a voice close behind him. Not to him, but Douglas.

'Stop! Don't take the car to that petrol lorry!'

Bouchet whirled round and stared at Fontenoy in a mixture of horror and surprise. 'What are you talking about?'

'Yes,' called Jim. 'Why shouldn't we put fuel in the tank?'

'Because I have filled it this morning. So that you could go straight off into the race. Va – va – va – voom!'

Jim smiled and waved his thanks; the Inspector turned and shook his head in disgust and walked slowly towards the refreshment stand. He needed a cup of coffee more

than anything else in the world – except for the diamond
itself.

Several moments later a hand tapped him on the
shoulder and nearly caused him to drop the paper cup.

'Fontenoy, what is it now?'

'Inspector, I can see you are a tired and worried man.'

'I am not! It . . . '

'I understand. It is the responsibility of finding the
world's most expensive diamond. But that is what I
wanted to talk to you about.'

Fontenoy stopped and looked in both directions – not
at once.

'What is it, Fontenoy?' asked Bouchet wearily. 'Can't
it wait?'

The great detective looked round again, then moved
closer. 'I was thinking, sir . . . I know it is a long shot . . .
what we detectives call a hunch, eh, sir? . . . but suppose
there was a connection between the men who attacked the
little car and the men who stole the diamond?'

Bouchet felt a nasty cold wave topple over his shoulders
and run down his back, as if somebody had poured the
coldest of water from a large jug.

'Wh . . . what did you say, Fontenoy?'

'I was thinking, sir . . . what if the men who stole the
diamond had hidden it in the car?'

'What?'

'I suggest, sir, that we should have our men search the
car immediately.'

Bouchet squeezed his hands together in a moment of
high emotion. The paper cup crumpled to nothing and
the coffee ran down his hands and along his arms. The
young detective stared at his hero in disbelief – could it
be that this great man, the finest detective in France, was
cracking up?

He saw the man's face start to crumple like the paper

cup had done; saw the hands start to shake – no, he could not believe it! Not him. Not the great Bouchet. Some of the others may have come to the end of their careers. Sam Spade living alone in a hotel room in Detroit looking for Brigid O'Shaughnessy in every bottle. Philip Marlowe walking down one dark street too many in Bay City.

Those great detectives might come to an end – but not the man Fontenoy had worshipped since he had read his first press cutting as a child.

And nor was it so. Even while Fontenoy watched, the Inspector came round, his blood began to flow freely again through his veins, his figure regained its former stature and panache.

'It is impossible, Fontenoy,' he said with a voice filled with authority. 'A thorough search would take over an hour. And an hour of delay would cause Douglas to lose whatever chance he has left of winning the race – a race he has travelled half way across the globe to win.'

With that, Bouchet turned to the counter and took a fresh cup of coffee.

'Oh sir, how I admire your consideration. I understand now exactly how you are thinking.'

And such was Fontenoy's excitement at seeing Bouchet restored to his best form that he shook the great man's hand. Coffee dribbled over both of them, but only Bouchet noticed. Fontenoy was already hurrying away.

Bouchet stood there and watched Herbie roar off in his desperate chase to catch up with the other cars.

'What now?' said a voice from under the counter.

'Don't worry,' growled Bouchet.

'But . . .'

'It is all right, I tell you. We will have an even better chance in Monte Carlo. We can get the diamond back there.'

89

'We?'

Bouchet looked at Max on his knees. 'You,' he said with the firm tone that Fontenoy so admired. 'You. Or else. I need say no more, I think?'

Max gulped and scrambled away only to be replaced by Fontenoy, who, although short of breath from running, was standing up.

'Inspector,' he wheezed, 'you will be proud of me.'

'Why?' said Bouchet, fearing the worst.

'I have done what I know you were about to do yourself. I have notified Monte Carlo. They will search the car when it arrives.'

Bouchet said nothing; merely got another cup of coffee and, without attempting to drink it, poured it slowly on to the ground.

CHAPTER SIX

By the time the race had reached the outskirts of Paris, Herbie had picked up enough ground to be in touch with the stragglers. Bruno and Gilbert were among the front-runners, with Diane in the first dozen.

The country outside Paris settled into a calm expanse of wide fields and small woods which clustered together for company and often had farmhouses to their edges.

The road was wide and level, from time to time bordered by avenues of poplars. The cars flashed along, brightly coloured streaks between the brown and green.

After one avenue, the road was lined by a brick and stone wall which marked the boundary of a large country estate. It was at this point that Bruno, who had slipped back from the lead by some dozen places, looked in his mirror and saw Herbie.

At first he could not believe it. How had that stupid little car even started, never mind caught him up?

But Herbie it was, and closing fast. Bruno gritted his teeth and looked ahead to where the road forked sharply left. Herbie continued to move up, Jim thinking he would take Bruno on the bend.

The two drivers glanced at each other as they went into the bend and then, with a menacing expression,

Bruno let his car swing a foot to the right.

Just twelve inches but they were enough.

Jim knew he had lost any chance of controlling his car as soon as he felt the touch. Herbie went into a violent skid, tried to pull himself through it and straighten up again.

No!

A wall.

A gate.

A hedge!

Herbie crashed through wood and green foliage and careered along the green expanse of a steadily sloping field. The first disaster had been avoided; but the next?

'Jim, isn't that . . . ?'

'Sure looks like it to me.'

'But we're headed straight . . .'

'. . . for it.'

They were for it all right.

For at the end of the wide expanse of field was an almost equally wide expanse of water. Or, to put it another way, a lake.

Splash!!

Herbie took to it like a car to water. A bright array of bubbles burst from the surface of the lake, shimmered in the sunshine and were gone.

'Glug – glub – g – g – goo – glub!'

Which may not mean a lot to you reading this book – unless you are doing so in your bath with the aid of a snorkel – but to Wheely it was clearly Jim's way of saying 'Let's get the hell out of here!'

The which they did.

The two French fishermen, who had been dozing in their rowing boat, had been roused by the sound of Herbie's dive. Now they saw ripples coming closer to-

wards them, and were aghast at the appearance of a large helmeted head, which broke the surface only yards away from them.

'*Nom de Dieu!*'

Wheely's eyes bulged threateningly. The fishermen clung to one another in fright, their rods tumbling into the water. Wheely shouted something to them that they could not understand – it was enough. They sat down in their boat and began to row for the shore with desperation.

At last, Wheely saw Jim swimming away to the right and followed him.

Soon the two men were lying on the bank, spewing water in all directions.

'Where's Herbie?'

'There!'

The little Volkswagen ploughed through the lake like a sea monster shouldering its way on to land, and came to a dripping halt alongside the two Americans. He opened his doors and several gallons of water, half a dozen fish and an old Wellington boot poured out.

'Well,' said Jim. 'What are we waiting for?'

'Nothing.'

They jumped in, and Herbie headed diagonally across the field, towards where the lodge gate of the estate stood by the entrance to the road. As they got nearer, it became clear that all was not well: the ornamental lodge gates were shut, and Herbie showed no signs of stopping.

Jim and Wheely stuck their heads through their respective windows and yelled at the elderly gardener who was pottering in the hydrangeas nearby.

The old Frenchman looked up and saw Herbie heading towards the gate; he may not have understood what was shouted at him, but he could see the danger. With a turn of speed remarkable for one so venerable, the gardener pulled the gate open in the nick of time.

Herbie roared through, the wind of his passing blowing the old man's hat high into the bushes.

Herbie knew that somewhere up ahead was Bruno. He knew what the German had done to him, and he was determined to get his revenge.

The high peaks of the Swiss Alps jutted into the clouds like needle points. Their crests were streaked with snow. Every now and then the frozen tumble of a glacier glinted in the bright sunlight.

Wheely pointed out of the window, his voice strained thin with amazement. 'We're going to take this little thing over that lot?'

'No, this little thing's going to take us.'

'You think Herbie can do it?' whispered Wheely, not wanting the car to be offended.

'You bet,' Jim laughed. 'The way Herbie's flying, nothing could stop him. And that includes the Himalayas.'

Wheely wasn't about to disagree – but there were two who were! High above the road in the foothills of the Alps, a helicopter hovered over a small plateau of rock. The rotor blades slowed and the machine made its descent. Two men disembarked; men bent on a dangerous mission: Max and Quincey. They hurried across the plateau to the hired car which awaited them.

They got into the car and drove carefully towards the main road, which was carrying the Trans-France cars.

Max parked the car around the bend and Quincey jumped out, hurrying towards the road sign which directed the race traffic. He turned the sign to point, not along the main section of road, but on to a smaller, narrower track which wound round the mountain.

Only five minutes later Herbie powered up the slope

towards the sign. Quincey was standing close to it with a clipboard, pretending to be marking off the cars.

Jim slowed down slightly, long enough for Quincey to look up and smile and point in the same direction as the sign. Jim nodded and waved his thanks and sent Herbie up the track.

As soon as the little car was out of sight, Quincey restored the sign to its original position and hurried to where Max was waiting. Now for the next part of their plan.

Herbie was soon on a narrowing, winding one-lane road with the granite mountain close on one side and a sheer drop on the other. Wheely was checking his map with an air of desperation, while Jim did his best to keep the car on the right track.

A steep hairpin bend appeared and Herbie's wheels came close to the edge – too close for comfort!

No – not again!

The second bend was even more dangerous than the first.

'Where are we, for heaven's sake?'

Wheely turned the map upside down, but it didn't look any better. 'Wherever we are, it's not on this map, I'm certain of that much.'

'Okay. I'm going to stop.'

Herbie came to a standstill, wheels almost touching space.

'Maybe we should ask directions?' suggested Wheely.

'Who from? A passing mountain goat?'

'There must be somebody.'

Wheely opened the door to get out. He swung his leg round and set his foot on the ground – only there was something missing. The ground wasn't there!

He pulled his leg back in and looked down through the open door: a sheer drop of thousands of feet. Wheely

gulped and sat back, reaching up to open the sun roof instead.

'Maybe I'll call from here.'

He stood up and swivelled his head around, finally putting his hand to his mouth in a Swiss-style yodel. 'Yo – da – lady – hoooo.'

For seconds there was nothing – then 'Yo – da – lady – hoooo.'

'See!' Wheely exclaimed. 'There is someone there.'

'Listen,' said Jim, and made the same sound, waiting for the same response.

Wheely was crestfallen, then pleasantly surprised. 'I never heard a real echo before.' After which Wheely made several other attempts at Swiss yodelling, breaking off in the middle for a hasty chorus of *I Remember You.*

Echo followed swiftly on echo, the whole thing building to a vivid crescendo of sound. As this reached its climax, a new and entirely different noise growled up from underneath it. The final strains of Wheely's echo faded away to be replaced by a tremendous rumbling. As the rumbling continued and grew in intensity, both the car and the ground underneath it began to shake and quiver.

'What's happening?' gasped Wheely as he was thrown from one side of the car to the other.

'It's you and your voice! I always said a voice like yours could move mountains.'

With that, Jim grabbed at the handle of the sun roof and slammed it closed only seconds before the first rock bounced off Herbie's roof.

The two Americans crouched on the floor until the small avalanche had ceased. When Wheely did dare to peer through the windscreen, a smile came to his lips.

'See,' he said. 'I did bring somebody after all.'

A large black sedan came slowly around the bend

and stopped only a foot away from them. As Jim and Wheely watched, Max and Quincey got out of the car and began to walk menacingly towards them. Quincey moved his right arm towards the inside of his coat and when his hand re-emerged, it was holding a gun.

No traces of a smile lingered on Wheely's face.

'You fetched someone all right,' said Jim. 'They're the ones who were after Herbie!'

And Herbie knew it!

The water squirters in front of his windscreen adjusted themselves like moveable gun turrets, one covering the neatly dressed figure of Max, the other the shambling shape of Quincey.

'Keep back!' cried Jim uncertainly.

'Yeah,' said Wheely. 'One more step and . . . '

'Oh yes?' snarled Max.

'Says who?' growled Quincey.

Herbie shot them right between the eyes! Swift and strong, streams of water jetted into their faces, causing both men to stumble backwards and Quincey to almost lose his grip on the gun.

Herbie's back wheel span as he started backing along the road, sending stones and pebbles skittering down the mountainside. Max and Quincey rushed to their car and leapt in – at least, they tried. On a road that narrow it wasn't easy.

Herbie was still backing feverishly along the road, but fate seemed to be against him. A large rock blocked his progress!

Jim and Wheely were jostled heavily forward by the impact. Herbie continued to bash his bumper against the rock, trying to dislodge it. Max and Quincey had finally got into their car by the time Herbie had freed his way backwards. Seeing the two thieves advancing, Wheely opened the sun roof and pushed his head through.

Jim looked up at him anxiously. 'What are you doing?'

'If it worked once,' Wheely grinned, 'it may work again.'

And he started to yodel. Midway through his second burst the familiar rumbling started. In the sedan, Max reached for one of his indigestion tablets and was just about to swallow it before he realised that this was something different.

The next second an avalanche of boulders came tumbling down upon the sedan, burying it, while Herbie backed happily away.

Neither Jim nor Wheely could hear what Max and Quincey were saying inside their car, but one thing was certain. It was not pleasant.

Although they were badly shaken by their bumpy detour and despite the fact that they had lost valuable time, Jim and Wheely were happy to be back on the Trans-France route once more. One thing alone bothered Jim. He thought there was a knocking in the fuel tank.

But when he suggested this to Wheely, the mechanic was insulted.

'Just take it easy, will you? You concentrate on the driving and leave everything else to me. There may be knocking, but not in my tank. Never!'

'Sounds like something's clunking around in there.'

'All right,' said Wheely, getting angry, 'we either listen to the driver and stop and take the petrol tank apart, or listen to the mechanic and try to win the race.'

Jim nodded, smiling. 'Okay, Wheely, I'm listening to the mechanic. Let's go, Herbie!'

Herbie reared up on his rear wheels like a wild stallion eager to stretch into a gallop. During the next hour he caught up with and passed car after car, their drivers staring at the blur as the little car speeded by them so fast they could hardly recognise what it was.

Before long, Herbie had Bruno in his sights. The German driver was amazed when he saw the Volkswagen in his rear-view mirror. Amazed and then annoyed. But before he could think of a scheme to get Herbie off the road once more, the little car had drawn alongside and obviously had the speed to pass him.

Bruno and Jim glared at one another – not for the first time – and Wheely chuckled aloud with delight. They were going to show that European! They were . . .

'What's wrong, Jim?'

Jim looked puzzled. 'Search me, but something sure is.'

The power was fading; he pushed his foot down on to the accelerator and nothing happened. There was no response. The engine felt jerky; it coughed like someone with a bad cold. Someone whose strength was failing fast.

Wheely looked desperately along the dashboard. 'The oil pressure's right up there . . . plenty of petrol.'

'You sure?'

'Sure I'm sure! But one thing's certain. However much petrol there is, Herbie's not getting it.'

Jim glared across at Wheely as Herbie fell behind the German machine. Bruno grinned evilly back over his shoulder and waved mockingly as the little car came to a stuttering halt at the side of the road.

Jim and Wheely jumped out of the car and as they did so they both heard the sounds of a helicopter overhead.

'That sounds like the Trans-France wrecking crew. Looking for machines that have dropped out of the race.'

Wheely shook his fist into the air. 'Back off, you vultures. I can take care of this.'

Other cars raced past them as Wheely began to examine Herbie to see what had gone wrong.

'I hate to mention it again,' said Jim, 'but I did hear a knocking.'

Wheely rounded on him sharply. 'You mean that nonsense about the petrol tank? Well, let's get it straight once and for all who the mechanic is around here.'

Wheely pulled off the petrol cap, placed it on top of the car and then rolled up his sleeve. He pushed his hand and then his arm into the tank, groping around inside it.

'You say it's the petrol tank and I say it isn't the petrol tank. See? It isn't the petrol tank . . .'

And with a look of triumph, he pulled back his hand with something inside it.

' . . . It's this rock that was *in* the petrol tank. So there!'

Wheely flung back his arm, preparing to throw the rock as far as he could. Jim gasped and grabbed for the flailing arm.

'Hey! What's going on here? You don't have to get all rough with me. I was only going to throw this silly rock away.'

'Some silly rock! Just take a look at it.'

Wheely put down his arm, put his hand in front of his face and opened his fingers. Very slowly.

'See! There's only one kind of rock that glistens like that.'

'Okay. So it's a piece of quartz. You can find millions in any quarry.'

He reared back his arm and prepared to throw the stone away for the second time. For the second time, Jim stopped him.

'You may find a lot of rocks but not one that's worth six million dollars.'

He took the stone from Wheely's hand and held it up to the sun. It sparkled and glistened like a star.

'But that's like . . .'

'. . . a star?'

'Sure.'

'So it is. *L'Etoile de Joie*. The Star of Joy!'

Wheely blinked. 'That's really the . . . But that's the biggest hunk of diamond I've ever seen in my life!'

'Yes. But how did it get here?' Jim asked.

Wheely's face was more blank than usual.

Suddenly an idea struck Jim. 'The black limousine.'

'Where?' gasped Wheely.

'No,' said Jim, 'not now. I meant they must have something to do with it.'

'You don't think . . . ?'

'I do. They're the ones who robbed the museum. They weren't trying to knock Herbie out of the race, they were trying to get the diamond out of Herbie.'

'And thank you for helping us,' said Max's voice. 'Up with the hands, please.'

Jim and Wheely turned fast. Max and Quincey stood facing them, Max with his gun drawn. Jim and Wheely glanced at one another, annoyed that in their excitement they had allowed the two villains to sneak up on them. But there seemed no alternative but to put their hands up.

Max smiled. It was not a nice smile.

'You gave us the slip for the last time,' said Quincey in a growl.

'We'll take that rock,' Max gestured with his gun.

Jim and Wheely backed away, the diamond tight in Jim's right hand.

'The rock!' snarled Max, his trigger finger whitening as the pressure increased. He held out his left hand towards Jim. 'Let's have it!'

Crash!! Crash!!! Suddenly the air was shattered by the sounds of gunfire. Max and Quincey ducked instinctively, glancing around to see who was shooting at them.

Crash!!!

Herbie's exhaust backfired again. Jim lunged forward at Max and knocked the gun from his hand. The two of them fell to the ground grappling with each other. Quincey rushed towards them, but Wheely grabbed at him and tried to throw him with a judo hold. Quincey laughed, straightened his arms and picked Wheely off the ground. He twirled the hapless mechanic about his head, faster and faster, finally flinging him several yards through the air.

Jim and Max were still struggling, the gun lying some feet away from them. Quincey hurried over towards Wheely and knocked him down just as he was trying to get up. He swung back his foot, intent on putting the boot in.

It was too much for Herbie. He rolled up behind Quincey and pushed him down a small ravine.

Wheely jumped painfully to his feet. 'Thanks, Herbie. That's just what I was going to do . . . as soon as I got up.'

At that moment Jim drove three straight lefts into Max's jaw and crossed with a stinging right. With a shout of pain, Max staggered sideways but, unfortunately for Jim, he fell close to the gun.

Jim moved fast but Max moved even faster. The barrel of the gun was levelled at Jim's chest and the look in Max's eyes was enough to kill. Again, the finger tightened on the trigger.

Dringgg!!!

The alarm on Max's pocket watch had come to the rescue yet again. Max looked down for only a split second, but it was enough. Jim dived full into the crook's stomach, the force of the blow driving all the wind out of him. They rolled over and Jim leapt to his feet, pulling Max up by his collar. Two swift right jabs and Max was down again; this time for keeps.

Jim picked him up and rolled him down into the ravine next to Quincey.

'Well,' said Wheely, 'we sure took care of that. Now what will we do with them?'

Herbie's hood opened and there, staring up at them was a coil of rope.

'Right, Herbie,' winked Jim, 'we'll tie them up.'

CHAPTER SEVEN

Everything was happening.

In the race, Diane Darcy had driven her Lancia into the lead and was holding off a determined challenge from the favourite, Bruno Von Stickle. Bruno had got away from the challenging pack and was in fourth, no, third place and closing fast.

Herbie was back on the main route and once more threading his way through the straggling cars and trying desperately to catch up with the leaders.

Max had struggled to the helicopter, despite having his hands and feet tied. He knocked the phone from its receiver and talked into the private line.

'Hello! Hello! Double X? Thank God you're there! No, we haven't got the diamond. No, we haven't got the car. Yes, I do value my life. But listen, Double X, one thing is certain. The goods will be in Monte Carlo in a couple of hours. There's no way to stop them getting there.'

Max heard the phone slammed down at the other end. He wasn't sure what the master criminal would do – but the master criminal himself was certain. If the diamond was going to arrive in Monte Carlo, then so was he.

'Give me the airport!' snapped Inspector Bouchet into

the telephone. 'And be quick about it!'

Still the race went on, now in its final stages and with Diane still in the lead and Herbie chasing hard. The road was twisty and lined with firs along one side, the other being open on to fields of fruit trees and vines, stretches of grassland and here and there a river.

A river!

'Hey, look!' called Wheely.

'Wow!' cried Jim. 'Isn't that the Lancia up ahead?'

Wheely peered through the open window towards the side of the road. 'Sure is.'

The Lancia had come off the road on a bend and had become partly submerged under water. From the angle they were approaching, neither of them could see any sign of Diane whatsoever.

'Maybe we ought to stop . . . ' ventured Jim, without actually slowing down.

'Stop?! And throw away a hundred thousand and the chance of our lives?! We've got it made if we carry on – now that car's out of it.'

'But she's in trouble . . . '

'Plenty of cars get into trouble. Let the rescue boys bail her out.'

'But the water looks deep,' said Jim, slowing down. 'She could be in real danger.'

'You're not . . . !'

'Sorry, but I am. The comeback comes second!'

Jim tried to turn the wheel to take the car off the road, but it wouldn't budge.

'Herbie doesn't seem to agree with you. He's just buzzing along.'

'That's because of that pack of lies you told him. If he knew that the Lancia was waiting for him to come before she'd start, then he'd behave differently.'

'Ssshhh!' hissed Wheely – but it was too late.

The steering wheel pulled right out of Jim's hands as Herbie headed for the sinking Lancia, making the fastest U-turn known to man!

'I hate to say this, Jim, but the trouble with your big mouth is that sometimes I think it's almost as big as *my* big mouth!'

Herbie came roaring up to the bank and skidded wildly to a halt, throwing Jim and Wheely all over the place. As soon as they had recovered themselves, they jumped out.

The front end of the Lancia was under water and slowly sinking into the ooze near the bank. They could see Diane now, trapped behind the wheel. With the water level rising inside the car, she was in real danger. And from the way she was struggling with the door it was obvious she was trapped inside.

'We'll get you out!' called Jim.

Diane opened her mouth to say something, but swallowed water instead.

'Keep your mouth shut for once,' said Wheely uncharitably.

'Come on!'

Jim and Wheely clambered down the bank and into the water. They pushed and pulled at the door and freed it just as the level of the water was approaching Diane's nose.

At the last possible moment, they pulled her clear and dragged her up on to the bank.

'Thanks,' said Diane, when she had recovered her breath.

'You okay?' Jim enquired anxiously.

'I think so,' she said, a little uncertainly.

'What happened?'

'I missed a gear and lost control.'

Jim nodded thoughtfully and glanced towards the water. 'You could have lost a whole lot more than that.'

But just because Diane had been rescued, that didn't mean that they could get back on with the race. There still remained the Lancia. Herbie backed up to it and locked bumpers. He moved into reverse gear and started to pull the Lancia out of the mud, his wheels spinning on the wet earth.

'Herbie, there's no time!'

'Forget it. He's going to get his girlfriend out of the mud.'

Behind them, Gilbert's car roared along the route to Monte Carlo.

'And us out of the race,' said Wheely gloomily.

With a final mighty effort, Herbie pulled the Lancia to safety.

Diane shook her head, astonished. 'I saw it, but I don't believe it.'

Bruno's car powered along the road past them.

'Well, you can believe this – we're now out of the money.' He pointed a finger at Jim. 'Because sometimes a comeback comes second!'

'Who's giving up?' said Jim, 'not me! Come on, Diane, you're coming with us.'

Diane shook her head. 'Thanks, but I'm staying with my car.'

Wheely nodded at Herbie. 'Looks like we're *all* staying with her car.'

Herbie's engine was off and he was alongside the Lancia, looking as if the last thing he wanted to do was go anywhere else.

From overhead came the sound of a helicopter. Jim and Wheely looked up, alarmed, thinking it might be the thieves. But the helicopter was clearly marked

'Trans-France Rescue'. It had spotted them and was moving in to land.

'The rescue guys will take care of us,' said Diane. 'We'll probably be in Monte Carlo before you are.'

'You and everybody else,' said Wheely, 'he's not going any place.'

Diane winked at Jim and walked across to Herbie.

'Herbie, listen to me,' she said softly, 'I know just how you feel. And I also know you're not a quitter. Now get out there and show them what you can do. Win it for them, Herbie . . . and for her.'

The Lancia's horn sounded weakly. Herbie's engine started with a roar. Wheely ran for the car door, while Jim turned to Diane, not knowing what to say.

'The rest is up to you,' she said.

Diane stepped forward and quickly kissed him on the cheek. 'Good luck.'

Something inside Jim was close to breaking point. But in his world there was a time for everything – and the time for Diane was not now. He nodded quickly and climbed into the driving seat.

The car swerved away from the bank and back on to the road. Time was tight. Herbie raced on and neatly overtook Booker's MG at the next bend. The first of many before the finishing line would be in sight.

Inside the central office of the Monte Carlo police, the police chief was seated behind his desk listening to the commentary on the radio. It seemed that the little American car was making a last ditch effort.

There was a knock at the door and the policeman looked up with surprise to see his old and respected colleague from Paris, Inspector Bouchet. He stood up and shook him warmly by the hand.

'Good to see you, Bouchet, but what are you doing here? Is your visit business or pleasure? I didn't know you were a motor-racing man.'

Bouchet shrugged. 'A little unfinished business.'

'You mean the diamond business?' The police chief frowned.

'Exactly so.'

'My friend, you wound me. You think I cannot handle a little search. Five of my best men are waiting for the cars to reach Monte Carlo.'

'I am sure your men know what they are doing, but . . .'

The police chief smiled. 'I see, my friend, you are afraid I will steal some of your glory.'

'There is no glory to be stolen. I wish to prevent a terrible mistake. The search is off.'

'Off!'

'Certainly,' Bouchet said. 'The message was an error by an over-zealous young detective, anxious to make a name for himself overnight.'

'This I can understand. But for news of that sort they invented the telephone.'

Bouchet's control was so good that it was almost impossible to see him flinch. 'The young man was under my personal command. Who knows what complications could arise from a situation like this? Even an international incident. I thought I should attend to matters myself.'

'Yes, wiser heads are always called upon to clean up the mistakes of the young.' The police chief touched a hand to his immaculate silver hair and Bouchet found himself wondering if it were a wig.

'For us,' the police chief continued, 'the rewards are in heaven.'

'Or a little sooner,' mused Bouchet. 'Or a little sooner.'

Crowds were thronging the narrow streets that marked the approaches to Monte Carlo. The sun shone on the red roofs of the houses and made even the green leaves of the trees glow with something close to fire.

Fire was the right word for Herbie. There were only two cars now left in front of him. Those of Gilbert and Bruno. Yard after yard, foot after foot, the three drivers clung to the distance they had earned with every ounce of skill they had ever learned.

Then – dramatically – for one of them the race was over. Gilbert pressed his foot on the accelerator, there was a snapping sound, a moment in which he held his breath and everything inside him seemed to die and the car slowed to the side of the road – dead.

Which left Bruno and Herbie.

Von Stickel was determined not to lose to the despised little American car at this stage. He moved his Lazer GT across the road and blocked every possible space through which Jim could have tried to force Herbie.

The road became a switchback and both cars seemed to leave the surface altogether at every hump. First Bruno, then Jim fought as their cars went into wild skids – both succeeded in controlling them.

'The dirty road hog!' shouted Wheely. 'Why doesn't he learn how to drive?'

'He knows how to drive, all right,' said Jim with a grimace. 'That's the trouble.'

The crowd thickened as they neared the finish; they waved and let off balloons over the two leaders. There was a hairpin bend and then a tunnel . . .

'If we don't get him by the tunnel, we're licked,' declared Wheely.

Jim nodded, agreeing. After that it seemed hopeless. Their effort would have been too late.

Both cars came out of the hairpin and changed gear

at the same moment: but Bruno was still in front. On the way to the tunnel he swung his motor from side to side across the narrow street, knowing that the race was already in his pocket, and his name already about to be engraved on the trophy.

He glanced in the mirror and grinned.

The next moment they were in the comparative darkness of the tunnel – a tunnel which was only one car wide!

'There's no way we can pass him,' said Wheely.

'Bruno was right. They never come back.'

Jim slumped back in the driving seat, but suddenly the steering wheel was plucked from his hands by a turn to the right. Herbie started going up the rounded wall of the tunnel, higher and higher towards the ceiling. Jim and Wheely were only held in place by their seat belts and their fear.

What was happening?

Bruno looked again in the mirror. Where was the stupid car? He had fallen so far behind that he wasn't even in sight any more!

Bruno laughed aloud and as he did so heard some faint sound above him. He shrugged – it could be nothing that would stop him at this stage. Ahead the light at the end of the tunnel came closer and closer.

My God! What was that? What *is* that? Upside down and driving along the tunnel roof – *ahead of him*!!

Herbie!

The Volkswagen swerved down to the ground just before the end of the tunnel and took the last few yards of darkness well ahead of its rival.

Bruno's face was glazed over: his will to win had been sapped by Herbie's extraordinary behaviour. The finishing line was in sight. Crowds, officials, reporters, photographers, television cameras – when they saw Herbie in the lead they went wild.

The race of a lifetime. The race of a decade. Of the century, even.

Herbie ploughed through the final straight and took the winning flag. Bruno finished fifty yards and many broken years behind; a ruined man, his confidence in shreds.

For Jim and Wheely it was different. They glowed with the beauty of their own triumph. Rejoiced in it. And there were so many to help them share the moment and make it one to savour for ever. When they got out of their car they were surrounded by fans who hugged them and finally lifted them shoulder high.

A bottle of champagne was opened and glasses produced. Jim and Wheely drank a toast to their own success!

For the best part of half an hour there were reporters clamouring for interviews. Jim and Wheely told the story of their sensational win to television viewers and radio listeners not only in France, but throughout the world.

Finally they were too tired for any more.

'I feel pooped!' said Wheely, as they moved off towards their hotel.

Jim nodded. 'Like it says in the song – "too pooped to pop".'

'You can say that again.'

'Sure. And there's one other little matter.'

'What's that?'

Jim patted his pocket.

'Oh, no!' exclaimed Wheely. In all the excitement, he'd clean forgotten that they had in their possession the most expensive diamond in the whole world!

And at that moment they recognised a familiar cough. As they looked round, the shape of Inspector Bouchet detached itself from the crowd and came towards them.

The Inspector walked slowly, eyes fixed on the pair of Americans. As he got closer, he extended his right hand. 'Let me add my congratulations.'

'You will,' Jim smiled, 'when you see what we've got for you.'

'I found it myself,' said Wheely. 'It was right in Herbie's petrol tank. I guess if it hadn't been for us . . . '

Jim took the diamond carefully from his pocket and showed it to the Inspector.

'Is this what you've been looking for, Inspector?'

Inspector Bouchet gazed at the sparkling diamond. After so many disappointments it was almost more than he could do to believe that this really was the Star of Joy. His bottom lip quivered and his eyes glistened with anticipation. For a moment, he was speechless.

'It's had a rough trip,' said Jim. 'But luckily it's going to wind up in the right hands.'

Bouchet sighed and spoke softly: 'Indeed it is.'

The Inspector's hand reached out towards Jim's. He was anxious not to seem too eager. A few inches from touching the diamond, with his own fingers for the first time, a voice stopped him. A voice that he had come to dread ever since the case had begun.

It was Fontenoy.

'Don't know how we missed connections, Sir, but here we are.'

Bouchet's fingers froze.

Slowly, very slowly and with an air of desperation, he turned to face his wretchedly enthusiastic detective. He saw as well the curator of the museum, Monsieur Ribeaux. The gleam in Bouchet's eye had disappeared behind a cloud. For him, the Star of Joy glistened no longer, held no promise of paradise.

Fontenoy pointed to the diamond in Jim's hand. 'You

see, Monsieur Ribeaux? I knew the diamond would be found.' He took a pace towards his Inspector; there were almost tears in his eyes. 'It is an honour to be at your side in this moment of triumph, Inspector.'

Ribeaux was beyond mere words. He grabbed the Inspector and kissed him on both cheeks.

'And I have more good news, sir,' piped Fontenoy. 'The two thieves have been captured.'

Bouchet clung to his last vestiges of self-control. 'Good, good,' he said, almost convincingly. 'Then, I would say the case is concluded.'

Jim, however, was still puzzled – surely there had to be more to it than this. Surely there had to be a plan. Surely...

'Look, Inspector, I don't want to interfere but you don't really believe the robbery was simply the work of those two hoods who ended up being outsmarted by Herbie? It seems to me that there must have been a mastermind behind all this...'

' ... or that museum had some pretty lousy security.'

Ribeaux choked back his anger, but Fontenoy, as usual, was more outspoken. 'Sir! Men have been challenged to a duel for less. The museum security was virtually foolproof. From the sensitised floor through the radar beams surrounding the pedestal to the very pillow on which the diamond rested – all the traps were conceived and executed by one man, and one man only.'

Fontenoy paused for breath, beaming. Bouchet touched his arm, trying to restrain him.

'Oh, no, sir. You are too modest. Credit where credit is due. The combinations to the entire security system were devised by you, in such a way that no one could have cracked their code. A superb feat of security!'

In the middle of the little group, Bouchet was staring towards the ground: feet of clay.

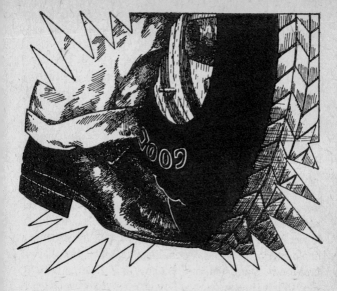

No one moved or spoke for what seemed minutes. It must have been seconds.

'The only person ...' Ribeaux mused.

'The only ...' murmured Jim.

'Which means ...' said Wheely.

'Which means ...' said Jim, more loudly, staring at the Inspector.

'Who besides the Inspector knew the details of the combinations?' It was Fontenoy who voiced the thought they were all thinking, though his voice sounded strangely unlike his own – hollow, dull, disillusioned, his eyes wide in shock and disbelief.

Bouchet pushed past Ribeaux and drew his service revolver. With his left hand he grabbed the diamond away from Jim. 'My retirement has been delayed too long. I hope no one will be foolish enough to make a move.'

The Inspector began to back away, covering any attempt to stop him. Only there was one thing he couldn't cover.

Herbie rolled forward fast and brought his front tyre to rest on the Inspector's left foot. Bouchet struggled to pull himself clear, but it was no use. He jerked the gun towards Jim, threateningly.

'Move this ridiculous car, Douglas, or I shall be forced to kill you!'

Herbie's hood flew upwards and sent the gun spinning from the Inspector's hand. Wheely jumped forward and caught it as it came down. Nervously, he pointed it at the Inspector. Jim stepped forward and retrieved the diamond. Then, with a smile, he put Herbie's hood down. 'Even a mastermind can be outsmarted by *this* car.'

Bouchet's body shook with anger. He clenched his fists and took a step towards Fontenoy, as if wanting to pummel him to the ground. Fontenoy moved almost faster than the eye could follow and, with a tell-tale click, a pair of handcuffs were tight about the Inspector's wrists.

Fontenoy managed a smile. 'I always hoped you'd be present when I cracked my first big case, sir. And you are.'

Jim was not going to waste his night's celebration. He arranged to take Diane to the very best restaurant in Monte Carlo, where he wined her and dined her as a champion should. When the last glass of brandy had been drunk and the candles had burnt themselves slowly and romantically to darkness, Jim and Diane left the restaurant. They were walking close together, Diane holding his arm.

'I should have spent less time defending myself as a racing driver and more time acting like a human being – particularly a woman.'

Jim stopped and turned towards her; she was in his arms. 'Now is time enough,' he said. And then he kissed her.

When they finally approached the doorman to ask for their car, he was staring into space as if in shock.

'The little VW?'

'VW?'

'Yes, the white one with the 53 on the side.'

'Yes, yes. I know the car. It is the toast of all Monte Carlo.'

'Well, it's also our transportation, if you wouldn't mind.'

'I wouldn't mind, Monsieur. There is nothing I would like better than to help you. But the little car, he is no longer here.'

'It was stolen?' Interrupted Diane, alarmed.

'Mamselle, you will not believe this but . . . no, I cannot say it, no one will believe it. I do not believe it!'

'It's all right,' said Jim. 'I think I know what you're going to say.'

'You don't mean . . . ?' Gasped Diane.

'I think I do.'

'Your little Volkswagen, he was stolen by *another car*!'

The doorman took a flask from his back pocket and had a long swig. Jim and Diane looked at one another.

Jim spoke quickly. 'Now I know you finally accepted what Herbie could do, but you're probably not ready to accept the same thing about . . . '

'Why not! Giselle can do anything she wants to!'

'Giselle . . . ?!'

Diane smiled at him. 'We are very strong-willed, she and I.' And then, softly. 'Shall we make it a foursome?'

Jim signalled a taxi. 'Take us to the most romantic spot in Monte Carlo.'

The silvered waves lapped against the silent beach in the moonlight. Jim and Diane lay back on the soft sand, his arm around her, her head resting on his chest. Further along the beach Herbie and Giselle nestled close, their lights blinking off and on and their doors lovingly entwined.

It was the perfect picture. The perfect end to the story.

Nothing to interrupt, except a familiar voice from higher up the beach, where a man in a beret talked persuasively to the young French waitress beside him. 'Being chief mechanic is important, but I didn't exactly win the race *all* by myself . . . I did have a little help from time to time.'

If Herbie understood, he showed no sign of being offended. Neither did Jim. Their happiness was too complete to be disturbed.

NEL

21

YEARS

BESTSELLERS

T035 794	HOW GREEN WAS MY VALLEY	*Richard Llewellyn*	95p
T039 560	I BOUGHT A MOUNTAIN	*Thomas Firbank*	90p
T033 988	IN THE TEETH OF THE EVIDENCE	*Dorothy L. Sayers*	90p
T040 755	THE KING MUST DIE	*Mary Renault*	85p
T038 149	THE CARPETBAGGERS	*Harold Robbins*	£1.50
T040 917	TO SIR WITH LOVE	*E. R. Braithwaite*	75p
T041 719	HOW TO LIVE WITH A NEUROTIC DOG	*Stephen Baker*	75p
T040 925	THE PRIZE	*Irving Wallace*	£1.60
T034 755	THE CITADEL	*A. J. Cronin*	£1.10
T034 674	STRANGER IN STRANGE LAND	*Robert Heinlein*	£1.20
T037 673	BABY & CHILD CARE	*Dr Benjamin Spock*	£1.50
T037 053	79 PARK AVENUE	*Harold Robbins*	£1.25
T035 697	DUNE	*Frank Herbert*	£1.25
T035 832	THE MOON IS A HARSH MISTRESS	*Robert Heinlein*	£1.00
T040 933	THE SEVEN MINUTES	*Irving Wallace*	£1.50
T038 130	THE INHERITORS	*Harold Robbins*	£1.25
T035 689	RICH MAN, POOR MAN	*Irvin Shaw*	£1.50
T037 134	EDGE 27: DEATH DRIVE	*George Gilman*	75p
T037 541	DEVIL'S GUARD	*Robert Elford*	£1.25
T038 386	THE RATS	*James Herbert*	75p
T030 342	CARRIE	*Stephen King*	75p
T033 759	THE FOG	*James Herbert*	80p
T033 740	THE MIXED BLESSING	*Helen Van Slyke*	£1.25
T037 061	BLOOD AND MONEY	*Thomas Thompson*	£1.50

NEL P.O. BOX 11, FALMOUTH TR10 9EN, CORNWALL.

Postage charge:

U.K. Customers. Please allow 22p for the first book plus 10p per copy for each additional book ordered to a maximum charge of 82p to cover the cost of postage and packing.

B.F.P.O. & Eire. Please allow 22p for the first book plus 10p per copy for the next 6 books, thereafter 4p per book.

Overseas Customers. Please allow 30p for the first book plus 10p per copy for each additional book.

Please send cheque or postal order (no currency).

Name ....

Address ....

....

Title ....

While every effort is made to keep prices steady, it is sometimes necessary to increase prices at short notice. New English Library reserve the right to show on covers and charge new retail prices which may differ from those advertised in the text or elsewhere.